WHY WEEPS THE BROGAN?

Hugh Scott believes in the power of the sub-conscious as a creative force. When he starts a book, he may know only the title, but, as he says, "if I tried to think it out logically beforehand it would not work." *Why Weeps the Brogan?* certainly did work – winning the 1989 Whitbread Children's Novel Award and being shortlisted for the 1990 McVitie's Prize.

It was in 1984, two years after winning the *Woman's Realm* Children's Story Writing Competition, that Hugh Scott decided to give up his job as an art teacher and become a full-time writer. His first novel, *The Shaman's Stone*, was published in 1988 and several more titles soon followed. These include *Freddie and the Enormouse*, *The Haunted Sand*, *The Camera Obscura*, *Something Watching*, *The Gargoyle* and *A Box of Tricks*, as well as two stories for younger readers, *The Summertime Santa* and *Change the King!* (all published by Walker Books).

Hugh Scott is married with two grown-up children and lives in Helensburgh, Scotland.

Other books by Hugh Scott

WHY WEEPS THE BROGAN?

Written and illustrated by

HUGH SCOTT

WALKER BOOKS
LONDON

First published 1989 by Walker Books Ltd
87 Vauxhall Walk, London SE11 5HJ

This edition published 1991
Reprinted 1991

© 1989 Hugh Scott
Cover illustration © 1989 James Marsh

Printed and bound in Great Britain by
Cox and Wyman Ltd, Reading, Berkshire

British Library Cataloguing in Publication Data
Scott, Hugh
Why weeps the brogan?
I. Title
823'.914 [F]
ISBN 0-7445-2040-1

For my brother, Drew, with love.

My thanks to the men of
Helensburgh Fire Station
for information on
FIRE EXTINGUISHER.

Why weeps the Brogan?
It sleeps not,
It eats at the dining time,
speeding on plunging limbs,
gasping from the shadows
to rattle, step on step,
and feed beneath the dribbling blue bird.

A girl's head fell from the balcony, turning white as it dropped into the brilliance of the chandeliers.

It shattered on the floor tiles, scattering fragments towards the great stone pillars. The *crash!* faded along corridors, then ticked into silence.

In THE COFFEE SHOP, Gilbert sighed and rose.

"Eat your rolls while they're hot," ordered Saxon gently.

She glanced over the rail into CENTRAL HALL, regretting the broken head. "We'll do the brushing later. How many chairs?" She smiled as the silver coffee pot wobbled in Gilbert's grasp.

"Twenty," he said.

"Thank you, Gilbert," said Saxon. She used his name carefully lest she forget. "But twenty was TUES, and this is WED." Her smile opened into a grin, and she stared past Gilbert innocently, pretending to study the Picasso poster on the column at his back.

"You've changed them? When?"

Saxon laughed.

"Not during sleeptime!" cried Gilbert. "You walked in the shadows?"

"There's nothing to fear —"

"Nothing much!"

"You slept quickly, and I was here and back before you had turned over once. Now..." Her hand, strong for a girl's hand, led Gilbert's glance around the little space among the THE COFFEE SHOP's pillars. "How many chairs?"

She sat back, delighting in the warm roll and melting marmalade. The flavours comforted her, as though – in a time before memory – rolls and marmalade had special meaning. Perhaps she had dreamed.

"Eighteen," said Gilbert. "You have removed two."

Saxon swung forward across the table and pushed his hair behind his shoulders. She was pleased at being able to reach. She wondered if Gilbert, eventually, would be able to reach her across the table.

"We must tie it back," she said. "Before the brushing. It wouldn't do not to hear. Now..." She tried to think of another question, gazing beyond the circular tables, wiggling naked toes on the rubber floor; she glanced up the stonework of the pillars, and let her eyes roll around the arches. "Four pillars make THE COFFEE SHOP," she murmured automatically.

"Each pillar is one span wide," said Gilbert spreading his arms.

"A wider span than that," murmured Saxon.

"Three spans," chanted Gilbert, "between pillars, and eight blocks to the balcony —"

"The balcony is forbidden! Forbidden!"

"I'm sorry, Saxon."

"All right," said Saxon. "You may spread me a second roll."

"You may pour me a third coffee." Gilbert's lips, as red as the rims on the grey cups, smiled.

Saxon reached again and touched his forehead. Gilbert closed his eyes.

"Pax," she whispered.

He spread her roll. She poured his coffee.

"What is our other name?" asked Gilbert, startling Saxon.

"I can't remember," sighed Saxon. "Keep asking. It will return when my thoughts are loose."

"We do have another name?"

"I think so. Yes. There are so many unremembered things."

"We must be very old," said Gilbert, "to have forgotten so much."

"Perhaps," murmured Saxon, "we have been here for ever."

"Like the world?"

Saxon nodded. Her pigtail rustled on her back. "I don't feel as old as the world."

"Do you think the upper world is as large as ours?"

"It may be larger. Or it may go little further

9

than the balconies and heads..."

"And FRENCH IMPRESSIONISM! We can read the words by standing on the rail —"

"Don't speak of it!"

Gilbert hid his face over his cup. "Is your roll correct?"

"Yes. Thank you, Gilbert. And gone! Time for the brushing."

Gilbert's hair rippled, pale under THE COFFEE SHOP's lights, as he glanced across CENTRAL HALL at the shattered head.

"It is a long brushing," he sighed.

"We must find a tie for your hair. Come. We will exit through EGYPTOLOGY and return to the brushing."

She gathered their dishes on to a red tray. She tapped a plate on the table. Gilbert scattered crumbs and the children peered up against the brightness of CENTRAL HALL's chandeliers.

Something fell – but not a head – swooping, and perched on the rail between the pillars. Chirruping rang from the balcony. More swoopings dropped.

In ten heartbeats feathers and bright eyes smothered the rail.

Then one soft bundle fluttered to the table, and Saxon's smile burst with delight, as brown bodies chattered over the crumbs.

"Hello, house sparrows," said Saxon.

"Passer domesticus," said Gilbert.

Saxon carried the tray behind the counter with its glass case full of books; in the kitchen she washed the dishes in a metal sink and left them to drain.

"The sparrows need more food," called Gilbert.

"Yes," said Saxon. She slid open the bread tin. "Oh, I'll bake again!" Gilbert came, and she gave him the last two rolls. He ran back to the table.

Saxon dried her hands on a paper towel. She prodded up into the towel dispenser. "The towels are almost finished!"

"I'll remember," sang Gilbert from among chirrupings.

"Let's go," said Saxon. "Your hair must be tied!"

But she stopped.

Between two columns, cardboard boxes sat cheek to cheek, tight-packed to keep out crawling things. And the lids sloped inwards, stuck with Saxon's tape, a slide for spindly legs.

Gilbert trotted from THE COFFEE SHOP and stepped over the boxes.

He turned, looked carefully inside each one, and shook his head.

Then he paced soundlessly on the tiled floor; and Saxon checked that his dagger sat snug in its sheath, and his spear-thong hung secure from his wrist; his sealskin jacket and trousers were correct, with nothing to catch the weapons. She frowned at his hair. She should have tucked it into his belt. But they were on the move.

She glanced up at the arch above the boxes. EXIT was lettered in gold on the grey stone.

Her own weapons were correct. She jumped high over the boxes. Ten paces distant, Gilbert leapt on to the sarcophagus. Saxon waited as his eyes searched the floor. His finger came up and she walked to stand beside the cold shoulder of the sarcophagus, red granite, 700 BC, found near Thebes.

She gazed down the length of EGYPTOLOGY. Black and white tiles patterned into the distance. Glass cases, electrically lit, made shadows for ancient gods.

Saxon listened. She heard nothing, and glanced up at Gilbert. He waited her command. She nodded, and he jumped, with no more sound than air rushing in his sealskin.

He ran among the gods. Suddenly up! on to a wooden seat. He crouched on the seat, his head turning slowly, looking. His finger flashed.

Saxon padded, toes spread to grip the cool tiles. She stood on the seat with Gilbert. She glanced behind her at the body in the glass case; stiff as wood, smaller than Saxon, bandaged into a shapeless log, decorated in dull colours. *Mummy of a young woman*, said a notice. *1,600 BC Nile Valley*.

She gazed under an arch into the gloom of another gallery. On the arch ARMS AND ARMOUR. She saw no movement on the tiles, but metal men stood in glass prisons, their hollow faces shadowed in steel skulls; mighty arms poised. Some had no legs.

Gilbert reached down with his spear, touching the tip on a black tile, turning it, glinting, whispering metal on stone.

They waited.

The suits of armour watched from the other gallery. On the floor, tight between the pillars of the arch, boxes. But nothing stirred from the boxes.

Gilbert drew in a breath.

"I think EGYPTOLOGY is clear," he gasped.

A smile tugged open Saxon's mouth. She said, "Come," and they trotted, spears dipped to a finger's width above the tiles, wending among displays of pottery and timeless things of stone, passing more archways – at this side to ARMS AND ARMOUR, at the other, to MINERALOGY then PALAEONTOLOGY. And every archway was tight with boxes on the floor.

A glass door blocked the end of the gallery. The children approached their reflections, Gilbert as tall as Saxon's shoulder.

Saxon pushed through, and Gilbert faced the new place, while Saxon shut the door quietly and with care.

Carpet warmed her feet. Stacked chairs leaned in the darkness of this little room, chairs the same as in THE COFFEE SHOP. Beyond another door – with a glass panel – a bulb lit a staircase going down. On the panel, PRIVATE, STAFF ONLY.

"We're safe now," said Saxon.

They descended steps, stone-cold, into corridors sparkling with bulbs which shone, somehow, only on the carpets, leaving endless shelves and pillars hanging with shadow. Shelves solid with books.

JANITOR, said a door. They entered. Saxon opened a cupboard and lifted a ball of string. She

13

fingered her sealskin belt and found, in a pocket she had sewn inside the belt, scissors; she snipped the string and returned the ball to the cupboard.

The scissors dug tight around her thumb. She stared.

Scissors should be longer than her hand; with shining blades and green loops. These scissors were small even for Gilbert; flowers curled on the blades, and the metal sat dull, just silver, eighteenth century, Scottish.

Was this memory?

Was there a time when the world did not exist? Surely she remembered things being alive and moving?

She thought of the world; up one stone flight of stairs from where she stood, hundreds of pillars keeping the floor and roof apart; supporting the upper world.

Nothing moved in their world.

Except Gilbert, and the sparrows. And spiders.

And the Brogan.

She said, "Here." And Gilbert – paper towels under his arm – presented his back.

She plaited his hair, bound his pigtail-end with string, snipped the string, prodded the scissors into her belt.

"Thank you, Saxon." Gilbert bounced his pigtail by swivelling his head vigorously. "Should we bring more towels?"

"No. We need food."

"Food for the Brogan."

"There is no need to speak of it."

They left the room marked JANITOR. They

trotted, shoulders nudging, carpet rough on their bare feet; bookshelves passing.

(Once, they had dragged a book from a shelf, staggering under its weight, spreading pages almost a span wide – with pictures, and columns of print which they could read but not understand; asking "What is *bomb*, and *warhead*, and *missile*?" But they had no answers.)

They stopped at a metal door.

A red light on the door displayed words:

Irradiated Food Store. For Use Only During Atomic War. This Door Must Be Kept Shut At All Times. No Unauthorised Personnel. Severest Penalties For Intrusion. Check Door Secure And Sealed On Entering And Leaving. Any Temperature Variation Must Be Reported Immediately On Amber Security Phone. No Smoking.

The door opened heavily, cold on Saxon's palms; a siren pulsed, and she grinned at Gilbert's screwed-tight face.

They went through, concrete drawing warmth from their feet. The siren stopped as the door slowly shut itself.

Saxon shivered. "As if it could think," she said.

"I'll check the temperature," said Gilbert, and he ran among shelves. His voice rose shrill. "Correct! Do we need potatoes?"

"No," said Saxon. *Hum-click* said the room.

A sign on a door announced:

WARNING Automatic gas turbines. These turbines are fuelled by a source of natural gas beneath the museum. They require no maintenance. Do not touch. 240 volts.

"Flour," said Saxon. "Dried milk." She approached the freezer. "Venison?" The freezer's padded wall extended into the store. "No, it's too strong. Bring a trolley. We might as well stock THE COFFEE SHOP while we're here. Margarine…"

Gilbert came, paper towels bouncing inside a wire-walled trolley. "I've brought a tin of plums. Is that all right?"

"Plums… And cherries for a cake. If they don't sink."

"Will you bake today?"

"Yes. We need rolls and bread, anyway. Cheese. Lots of cheese. How I hate it." She pointed, smiling, at cardboard boxes in a corner. "Plenty of spider traps. Do we need toilet roll?"

"No. Cigars."

"Is that everything? We should have written a list."

"We only came to tie my hair."

"Then there's the brushing, Gilbert. The brushing."

They secured the door of the food store, and pushed the trolley along carpet; between walls of books, beneath fat pipes; pipes as fat as anacondas; as suddenly bending as anacondas when one would turn around a pillar, clinging to the black ceiling, vanishing into the pin-pricked darkness.

At the stone stairs, they lifted the trolley up to

They stared through the heavy glass door into EGYPTOLOGY. Gilbert gripped his spear in thrusting poise, the point low, the haft against the inside of his forearm, the loop on his wrist.

"It is clear," he insisted.

"They bite so horridly," whispered Saxon, and she rubbed the skin of her left hand.

Gilbert pulled the door.

"Take every care!" whispered Saxon. She gripped the trolley handle, her spear – secure on its wrist-thong – across the groceries.

They advanced, Saxon's bare heel letting the door shut gently. She glanced back. If it lay open the thickness of her finger...

With no more sound than a shadow walking, Gilbert paced to a pair of chairs – chairs from the little room behind the glass door, placed specially. He strode up, on to the further chair, where he crouched, still as a god. Then his finger rose, and Saxon leaned to move the trolley, pulling her cheeks tight at the muttering wheels.

On to the nearest chair she stepped, then Gilbert sped along the tiles. He signalled and Saxon raced, anxious as always at her spear not in her hand, following the trolley's weaving trail among the glowing cases, praying the wheels would run true and, oh! that click of metal! more work to silence it! running past gods who thought of nothing; your brains are stone! cried Saxon in her mind. What use are gods of granite and blind basalt who teach nothing for they know nothing...

17

On to! the wooden bench, hauling the trolley to trembling silence. Then Gilbert walked; and she walked, smiling under the arch to THE COFFEE SHOP; replacing the row of boxes once the trolley was through.

Then they packed the food into cupboards; loaded the towel dispenser; beamed without speaking, catching glances, Saxon grinning, then she simply had to say it!

"There are no spiders in EGYPTOLOGY!"

"No spiders!" beamed Gilbert.

"You understand the meaning? We can walk! We can sit on the floor!"

"Sleep on the floor!"

"We could! If we wanted! And, Gilbert…"

Gilbert's lips split into a smile.

"With more boxes from the food store, we can clear ARMS AND ARMOUR!"

She concentrated on shutting cupboards firmly.

"ARMS AND ARMOUR," whispered Gilbert.

"But now the brushing," said Saxon. "Put the cigars on a table for later."

"The cheese – "

"Not yet!" muttered Saxon, and she strode into THE COFFEE SHOP and stared out at the clock, square on a stone column in CENTRAL HALL, green numbers telling her, 8.57 WED. 4 YEARS 81 DAYS FROM HOSTILITIES. "It is not time!"

"Come," said Gilbert gently.

She followed him over the rail where the sparrows had swarmed. She dipped her blade to a finger's thickness above the floor. She watched the tiles, hearing the clatter of a brush handle, the hiss of bristles as Gilbert took a brush from behind the silver cabinet.

He went in front of her, sweeping a span-wide path through the fragments of the head.

"Marble," said Saxon, watching the sugary portions pushed into a line.

"You must be vigilant," warned Gilbert.

"Yes, Gilbert," muttered Saxon, and her spear swung, her eyes trying to penetrate the darkness of the black tiles, seeking well into the distance to the stone bases of the columns and the cardboard boxes that stretched between them. She turned. ARMS AND ARMOUR said a sign. SHOP said another. She turned. THE COFFEE SHOP, EGYPTOLOGY, ETHNOGRAPHY, EXHIBITION AREA, ENQUIRIES. She trotted, seeing boxes secure across every exit. She jogged in a circle, every black tile scrutinized. She ran around the orrery, a glass dome on a drum-shaped base of wood, tall enough to hide her from Gilbert, wide enough to make her sprint to get him in sight. Bolder she moved, outside the range of the scattered head, approaching a column, racing beside a row of boxes, air in her hair, pigtail swinging; past the great doors of timber and glass; ignoring the darkness beyond the doors, speeding, feet a beating blur, heartbeats a steady pulse, the spear-point a needle of death searching every rushing tile, every dusty corner.

She padded to a halt, smiling.

"Anything?" asked Gilbert.

"Nothing!"

She took the brush and Gilbert snatched her spear.

"Careful." She unlooped it from her wrist.

She smiled. Gilbert would search the boxes and count spiders in the INSECTICIDE.

Saxon walked over the scatter area. She looked hard at white tiles, because marble splinters hid there, like spiders on black.

"Two!" called Gilbert.

She nodded.

"Three, here!"

She met Gilbert at the pile of marble. A stone eye stared across the floor.

"Seven dead," said Gilbert.

"And none in CENTRAL HALL. Did you put them out for the others to eat? We must bring the AMMUNITION box." She gazed at the heap of sugared stone. "One day there will be no more heads to throw."

She dropped the brush and stepped towards THE COFFEE SHOP; she hesitated; Gilbert's spear jerked.

Above the chandeliers, something rattled.

"It's early," said Gilbert.

"Let it wait!" snapped Saxon, and she marched to the rail of THE COFFEE SHOP and was over and among the tables without a change in stride.

She reached under the counter and caught the rope-handle of a box. She pulled, and Gilbert crouched with her, and they carried the box – with a shovel inside – to the piled head. AMMUNITION was printed on the box's wood.

The rattle rang closer.

"It can wait!" said Saxon loudly, as if her voice

might rise above the lights.

She dug the shovel through the glistening stone, and crashed it into the box; she thrust again, turning her face from rising dust.

"It may drop another head," said Gilbert.

"Brush!" ordered Saxon.

Gilbert brushed, and Saxon held the shovel. Gilbert dabbed up splinters on his fingertips.

They lifted the box, rope rough on their palms, staggering, the shovel threatening to slide from the fragments.

"It's hard to believe it's so heavy!" gasped Gilbert. "Lower your side, please, Saxon!"

"Oh! We'll have to leave it! Down! How I hate that Brogan! Hate!" But she ran – over the rail and among the tables.

She jerked the fridge door and slid out the block of cheese. "Proceed!" she ordered Gilbert.

He leaned her spear against the sink. She watched him go around the counter; dagger safe. He lifted his spear from a table, and disappeared towards EXIT.

"Gilbert."

"Saxon." He was waiting only a step beyond the pillar.

"Pax. You may make my coffee. Afterwards."

"You may spread my roll."

Saxon smiled. She heard nothing, but Gilbert, she knew, was now on the sarcophagus searching the floor – just in case – for spiders.

She took a knife from a drawer, measured the cheese with her hand, and cut a lump.

"There's no bread," she muttered. "Well. It can

do without." She hesitated.

She reached for storage jars, unplopped plastic lids, tumbled figs on to a tray, poured raisins.

She placed the cheese on the tray.

She stared at the food, not seeing it, hating the thing she fed; hating having no bread.

The rattle swept close above the chandeliers.

She looped the spear to her wrist, lifted the tray, and stepped over the boxes under EXIT.

Gilbert was pacing freely along EGYPTOLOGY. He turned and spread his arms. The spear-blade glinted under spotlights. His shadow jigged as he danced, and Saxon ran, smiling.

"Two dead in the boxes!" claimed Gilbert whisperingly. His arms showed her all the floor of EGYPTOLOGY. "It is clear! Come!" And she followed him to an arch which read ARMS AND ARMOUR in gold.

Gilbert pointed the spear over the row of traps. Saxon stood still. On the tiles in ARMS AND ARMOUR sat two spiders, bodies like dry plums, in a spray of short hard legs; white INSECTICIDE among hairs. "Others will eat them, and die," said Gilbert. "Come!" he said again, and stepped beside the spiders.

Saxon was content to follow. Gilbert's skill with the spear was greater than hers. He could thrust five times a heartbeat and never miss.

She smiled back towards EGYPTOLOGY. Her idea with the boxes had succeeded. At EGYPTOLO-GY's far side, an arch led to PALAEONTOLOGY, where a distant display case, partly hidden by great skeletons and prehistoric monsters, touched her eye. The case was very dark.

"Saxon!"

Gilbert stood on the bottom step of a flight of stairs.

Saxon ran, the tray sharp in her waist, spear-tip searching. She made a little leap, up beside him.

"Your thoughts were loose!" hissed Gilbert. "There are spiders in ARMS AND ARMOUR!"

Saxon drew a breath to speak, but on the balcony, the rattling clattered close.

The children faced the stairs.

Saxon's heels felt very naked just two hand-widths above the tiles, but she knew the lip along the step was a barrier to spiders.

The steps rose to a landing. From the landing, one flight went left, another right.

Saxon tiptoed to the landing.

She put the tray on grit. The grit dribbled from the shattered beak of a blue bird. The blue bird was a stained-glass window, with Homer on the windowsill; Homer, bronze, nineteenth century; with grit slithering – now and then – over his face, and gathering among his lyre strings.

Saxon danced back, down the bottom flight, as the rattle slowed to a rumble.

Something passed behind the balustrade's little pillars.

Saxon raised her spear.

"Fifteen steps on the bottom flight!" gasped Gilbert.

Saxon joined in. "Thirteen steps to left and right!"

Rumble.

"Tiles dark as a spider's back."

Rumble, click.

"It's here!" whispered Gilbert.

Through the stone pillars of the banister Saxon saw the twist of a head. Shivers walked on her skin. She looked at her toes. "Why does it stare so!"

Clunk, on a step.

Breath with a voice in it.

Clunk.

"It's coming down!"

Fingers whitened on spears. Effort, as the thing moved behind the banister.

Clunk, on to the landing. Rags over something.

The children stood, hard as statues. Inside Saxon, hatred.

Hair, as fair as Gilbert's, cut to wrist length; curtaining the face; crunching on glassy dust to the food, but not walking; rolling as if on two wheels; knuckles propelling against the landing's tiles; and bones, dark as wood, projecting up the back, higher than the head. And dragging in the dust, feet, the soles up, and white.

It nuzzled the cheese through its hair.

A hand searched the tray, thick and ugly.

The head swung.

Saxon's heartbeat clogged her throat. She gasped. "There's no bread! Later! I will bring it later!"

The head twitched, and Saxon's glance went to the thirteen steps, then to whatever moved beneath the rags. She understood. "I will put it at the top of the stairs."

The head stayed.

Saxon thought an eye blinked.

Then feeding continued.

A hand put the last of the cheese into the rags. It gathered the figs and raisins, storing them with the cheese, carefully lifting raisins which escaped on to the dust.

It jerked the tray down the stairs with a clatter that startled the children; Gilbert turned his back and peered into ARMS AND ARMOUR.

The Brogan rolled across the landing. It placed its knuckles on the bottom step. Bare arms beneath the hair strained with muscles, making Saxon think of her own arms. The body was lifted on to the step. Panting.

"Is it clear?" whispered Saxon. She lifted the tray.

"Come."

A sound from the Brogan made her pause.

The creature steadied itself. A hand swept to its face, tipping an invisible cup, then gestured at Saxon; the arm was beautiful.

"You have water!" hissed Saxon. "You have! Do you not wash as we wash? Go! Go! We hate you!" Thrust with the spear, but daring not a pace closer to those bent and calloused fingers.

"Come!" hissed Gilbert, and they trotted, Saxon weeping suddenly, among the gods of Egypt.

Under the spotlights of THE COFFEE SHOP, Saxon stood by the rail gazing at the orrery and CENTRAL HALL's great doors of glass and wood. The debris of the girl's head glistened white in the AMMUNITION box.

"Coffee!" said Gilbert to her back.

"Thank you, Gilbert." She laid her spear on a table and sat with him. She pulled the cigar box under her face and enjoyed the fragrance of its wood; opened the box, enjoyed the cigars' scent. Gilbert used the edge of his hand to wipe aside crumbs left by the sparrows. Saxon chose cigars as Gilbert poured. She scratched a match on Swan Vestas and the sound rasped among the stone columns that stood close around; and the flame burst with energy on Saxon's eyes. Did this tiny light remind her of something just beyond memory's edge?

"It will be on the balcony," she said, and Gilbert stared blue for half a heartbeat as a rumble sounded loud, then suddenly fading, as if the Brogan had turned a corner.

"Why do you weep when we feed it?" asked Gilbert.

"Not every time," cried Saxon.

Gilbert's eyelids shielded his gaze.

"Not every time." sighed Saxon. "I hate it. And yet – "

The coffee slid around her tongue. Its warmth comforted her stomach. " – sadness lives in me, Gilbert. Where did it come from, that Brogan? Has it always been? Like the mummy? Like the armour and reptiles?"

She faced the rail again staring at the great doors and the balcony over the doors; with the organ filling the balcony; golden pipes as tall as pillars, but thin, and crowded like drinking straws.

Memory was a strange creature; strange as the Brogan; a hiding creature that lived in her mind's shadows, stirring sometimes from a deep sleep, but never wakening.

"What is beyond the doors?" She faced Gilbert.

"Nothing – "

"Beyond all the windows of the world – ?"

"Nothing!" Gilbert frowned, sucking his cigar. "Dust and darkness. You can see it through the glass of the doors. Beyond the blue bird is grit. Beyond everything is – "

He paused.

Saxon's head swivelled.

Hands leapt for spears, and they flew, those children, like sparrows, and perched on the rail; Saxon, her cigar angled between her teeth.

Distantly, a noise boomed.

Above the chandeliers rang alarmed chirping.

Glass broke far away.

The boom lingered.

Saxon touched a column.

"The stone moves!" she whispered.

Then the noise stopped, and its echoes fled, a giant sound, limping into the distance.

"Look!" cried Saxon. She pointed at the great doors.

"Is it smoke?" shouted Gilbert. "Smoke like a

cigar?"

Around the doors, brown explosions billowed into CENTRAL HALL.

"Dust!" said Saxon. "Run! Run! EGYPTOLOGY! Run!"

She spat away her cigar and twisted on the rail. She sped across table tops, through the arch marked EXIT, and raced on black and white tiles.

They stopped at the little dark room. They looked back.

A brown wall advanced; softly, it absorbed the wooden bench and the mummy. Sparrows flew out of it, curving through archways into ARMS AND ARMOUR. A green god, straight-backed with dignity, vanished slowly; and spotlights pinged in little frightened voices.

In the upper world, a rattle.

"Come," whispered Gilbert. He pushed the door. They went through. Then a smoky wall leaned on the outside of the glass. They shut PRIVATE, STAFF ONLY behind them and descended to JANITOR.

Saxon sat on a chair, feet off the floor. Gilbert plugged in a heater.

The smell of the dust reminded Saxon. Oh, it reminded her – she smiled – of the feel of sparrows; of pushing her fists into dough.

Gilbert crouched by her leg. "What is the meaning of the trembling?"

Saxon touched his head. "I don't know, Gilbert. But – " She breathed, trying to catch the taste of the dust again. "The world, Gilbert – "

Gilbert's mouth opened.

" – do you remember how vast it was before the spiders came? Do you remember the library? and how we ran on carpet paths, losing count, always, of the length of shelves?"

"I don't remember."

"Your legs were too short for real counting. Ten of my paces were fourteen of yours – "

"You have always been taller! It's no different now!"

"Gilbert, Gilbert! Once, you could not see over THE COFFEE SHOP counter!"

Gilbert's lips tightened, squeezing away the redness.

Saxon remembered he did not like change. She said, "The world is still vast. But when I smelled the dust it seemed, just for a heartbeat, that it extended far beyond the library, on and on, with a floor that dipped and rose, and the air moved, and the roof spread forever, bright – bright without lights, and no pillars supported it! And colours…! Oh, Gilbert! If only it could be real…"

"If only it could be real," said Gilbert.

A little laugh exploded in his throat. "But I think the roof would need at least a few pillars, Saxon."

She smiled; and thought of the Brogan. "Let us look upstairs."

Gilbert switched off the heater, and they returned to PRIVATE, STAFF ONLY.

In EGYPTOLOGY, lights hung in a brown mist.

"It's not as bad," said Gilbert.

"We shall wait," said Saxon.

* * *

Saxon stretched her arms, sealskin rustling on her shoulders. "It will be a great brushing," she said, and Gilbert groaned.

"It will take until SUN or MON," he complained.

"Longer, if the dust comes again – "

"Again!"

"Did you not say there is nothing outside but dust and darkness? The world could fill with dust." She stared at him.

His pale skin whitened, showing veins blue with blood. His head shook, bouncing his pigtail.

"It could. If there is only dust outside there must be plenty."

"No! God wouldn't allow it! He wouldn't make the world and destroy it! We haven't done anything wrong! Why should dust fall on us! It isn't fair!" Tears threatened.

"Calm, Gilbert." She held him, regretting her words; smelling the dust in his hair, the faint scent of tobacco. "I was being foolish. Do not weep. Have we not survived the Brogan? Have we not cleared the spiders from CENTRAL HALL? There is much to do before the world ends, and so much, Gilbert, still to learn! Do you remember ORNITHOLOGY before the lights went out? Can you recite case number two? The family Hirundinidae? Sand Martin. Swallow – "

"Red-rumped Swallow," whispered Gilbert.

"Correct… And the Fringillidae? What was the pretty blue and yellow bird you liked?"

"Citril Finch. I'm all right, Saxon." He eased free of her embrace. "You may find me something to eat."

"You may make my coffee – "

Saxon looked into EGYPTOLOGY.

The dust had sunk below the spotlights, but display cases still glowed in mist.

She sighed. "We will eat in the underworld. Come. It will be sleeptime before the air is clear."

"The Brogan will be annoyed," said Gilbert. "You promised bread."

"Perhaps the Brogan is dead."

They descended stone steps to the long corridors, striding in swelling shadows beneath bulb after bulb.

At their spear hands, a corridor stretched gloomily between shelves of great books.

They strode on, then hesitated, spears dipping, hands on daggers.

They stopped.

Gilbert moved to the corner pillar. He looked round it, and stepped back; then Saxon looked, the pillar's stone cold on her fingertips.

She knew not to gaze at the lights. She stared along the floor, wishing the carpet was not grey, because grey could hide spiders.

They have never been here, she told herself. There is no way down for them.

She saw nothing.

But something walked on her foot.

She leapt, and her spear thrust as if by its own thought, plop! as the body burst on the carpet. Plop! as another leggy thing sped from under the shelves.

Gilbert's spear glittered five times a heartbeat.

Spiders swarmed.

"Climb!" cried Saxon, and they clung among the books, spears dipping death.

Saxon paused to peer at her foot. She gasped with relief, then stabbed swiftly, turning the carpet from grey to red.

"We cannot stay here!" whispered Gilbert.

"We must kill them!" shrieked Saxon quietly. "Kill them! They may get to the food store!"

So they worked at killing.

While the spiders ran, seeking the quivering blobs, once family, now nourishment.

Saxon's left arm burned with the strain of holding on. Her fingers clung dead. She swept a glance along the shelves, but the shelves rose to the ceiling leaving no space where she and Gilbert could rest. Her spear danced.

Opposite Saxon, a metal bottle hung on the stone column that was the corner of the passageway. Many times she had looked at these bottles. Most were black, with FIRE EXTINGUISHER printed on them in white. But they were cold to touch and Saxon knew they contained no fire. Her spear darted like a steel snake. But a match contains no fire, she thought, until I strike it. Then she remembered instructions about pulling a pin and pointing at base of flame. She could never see a pin, and the other words were meaningless.

But her eyes returned again and again to the black metal cylinder on the column. Could it contain fire?

Then she saw the pin, and smiled grimly. She

hadn't recognized it as a pin because it was large, and looped at the top to put a finger in.

She eased her left hand. She would have to jump to the shelves across the corridor. And she had her back to them. She would have to jump, and turn, and find a hold, all in the space of a single heartbeat. And the shelves were more than a span away.

Her spear lanced down into the thickening layer of red and black, the dead and the feeding. She raised the spear, and reached across, thrusting it hard between books.

She leapt, surprising herself. She hadn't prepared. She didn't think. Twisting. Stretching round with her left arm and its stiff curled fingers, aiming her right hand towards an upright of metal, willing her feet high enough to speed on to the tops of books. Crash! Her feet slipped as the books burst down out of the shelf, splashing on the floor; her left hand couldn't grip, but her right fist clung to metal and her left arm went over the spear, and the spear went snug into her armpit, sagged, held, Saxon dangling, slammed breathless against the shelves, knees bent to keep her feet clear of the floor.

Her knee found a resting place. Her left-hand fingers moved – in two heartbeats she was safe and hauling FIRE EXTINGUISHER from the column. She pulled the pin, gripping tight on the handle.

But no fire spread death from this strange cylinder. Instead, from the horn which dangled on a thin pipe at the bottle's top, a blast of white mist struck the floor, and Saxon screamed in triumph, letting the horn swing, for below the blast the spiders' legs were blown off and their carcases rolled into a ridge of hardened pulp.

"Under the shelves!" howled Gilbert. "Under!" And Saxon descended cautiously, jetting death beneath the shelves where the spiders had appeared; cold death, for the horn chilled her palm and blood crinkled on the carpet like ice from the freezer –

"Turn it off!" cried Gilbert. "This way!"

She ran after Gilbert around the pillar to the other side of the shelves, and she sprayed, screaming, until nothing moved, and the mist ceased.

Suddenly.

She dropped the cylinder.

She allowed a smile to rise on her face.

Legs lay scattered, like bent matches from a hundred Swan Vestas. She prodded her dagger at a carcase, and the carcase broke, letting the insides flop out.

Gilbert stood poised, panting, eyes shining with victory. His pigtail shifted as his spear struck.

"It is finished?" gasped Saxon.

Gilbert's blade wandered low over the carpet.

"My spear is in the books," whispered Saxon, and Gilbert led her, and she followed, crouching, dagger light in her fingers, the tip a finger's thickness from the floor; round the great pillar, to the ridge of bodies in the corridor that led to the food store. They listened, but nothing lived.

Saxon jerked her spear from the books.

"We must look again," she said. "We must be

correct." And Gilbert's spear-tip whispered to the carpet, but no dark movement came to investigate. They returned to the other side of the shelves, sending the teasing noise into the shadows.

"There are no more," said Gilbert.

But still they waited, breathing, being certain.

Then Saxon spoke. "How did they come here, Gilbert? They have never been in the underworld."

Grit trickled, sparkling down from above the lights.

"Look!" Saxon's spear leapt, pointing at the black ceiling.

A crack in the ceiling, difficult to see.

"Watch the floor." And up the shelves she climbed, hair against that black ceiling, peering along above the lights, probing with the spear. Grit dropped.

"They could have come through," she said, and something moved in the crack and came out clinging to the spear's blade.

"Gilbert!"

She dipped the blade towards Gilbert, but the spider climbed, finding a grip in the patterns of the spear's haft, rushing towards her hand. She dropped the spear, snatching her hand away and Gilbert struck.

He passed the spear up as she descended.

"We must block the crack," she said.

"How?"

"We need something soft. I know." She rested her spear, and tugged at one of the great books.

She lowered it to the carpet, heaved back the cover and tore out pages. Then she crushed the paper and pushed her spear through it, and climbed, and prodded the paper into the crack. But it came away with the spear.

She thought. Then tried again, using the haft instead of the blade. The paper stuck in the crack. She stuffed it in firmly, then stopped. It wasn't enough. She climbed down.

"They could eat through it," she said.

Gilbert was taller, his eyes level with her mouth. He stood on the book on the floor; Saxon smiled. She leaned her spear on the shelves and hauled down more books, stacking them, dust rising, old dust, thin and ancient-smelling.

"What are you doing?"

"Building a pillar. God built pillars of stone. I am building a pillar of books." She worked, Saxon, until she was warm in this cold world, panting dust.

The column leaned, and she stood straight, resting. The thicker spines raised the stack higher at one side. She turned the books, one spine one way, one the other.

Then: "Twenty!" she gasped.

"Let me," said Gilbert. So Saxon held his spear and he struggled with a book in his arms until he laughed, letting it slip; then he frowned and placed it on the stack. He lifted more books until sweat shone on his temple; then he began a second column beside the first, and stood on it.

Saxon said, "Correct thinking," and gave him his spear; then she heaved up more volumes from the past, beginning a third column to let her reach the second. Then a fourth, and fifth.

At last the lights shone hot on her cheek, and one more book would jam the crack. She stared into the crack with its crumpled pages; nothing moved. But the column swayed and she embraced the top books, saying, "Oh! Oh!" until they steadied; then she descended her staircase.

"You do it," she asked Gilbert. "My arms are tired." And Saxon held the staircase with her body while Gilbert crept up, head among the lights, busy in shadows.

"There!" he said, and books fell, Gilbert sliding down the staircase, feet towards the lights, bump! Oh! turning to gape at the column, Saxon, reaching to him, but also gaping.

The column stood tight between ceiling and floor.

Saxon relaxed. Gilbert's face glittered with sweat. His pigtail hung over his chest, and the hair of his sealskin stood ruffled by the fall.

He said, "We must eat."

Water rushed on to Saxon's feet from the tap in JANITOR's sink. She rubbed her soles, watching the water run red with spiders' blood.

Gilbert, who had splashed his hands and face briefly, made sandwiches of corned beef and biscuits from a tin.

Saxon rubbed herself with paper towels then sat at the heater.

She bit her biscuits. "Thank you, Gilbert."

"What caused the trembling?" asked Gilbert.

Saxon shook her head and curled closer to the heat.

"Will it come again?" he whispered.

"I hope not."

"Do you think it caused the crack?"

"Of course!" cried Saxon. "Correct thinking! It caused the crack!"

"What is our other name?"

Dread rose in Saxon. For a moment memory struggled.

"I don't know." She held the biscuits to her lips. "I have never seen so many spiders."

She tried to think. "They came through the crack, from..."

"From the world," said Gilbert.

"But what part? If we go up the stairs, before us is EGYPTOLOGY, with ARMS AND ARMOUR on this side and PALAEONTOLOGY – "

"Is PALAEONTOLOGY above the crack?"

"I think so. Wasn't that where the spiders first appeared?"

"I don't remember. It must have been long ago."

"They restrict us, Gilbert."

Saxon stared at the orange-hot bar of the heater.

An idea stood at the edge of her mind.

"The black bottle, Gilbert. There is one in every archway. Gilbert? D'you think God knew the spiders would come, and gave us FIRE EXTIN-GUISHER?"

They returned to the heaps of spiders.

The spiders had softened and bled.

"We should shovel them away," whispered Gilbert.

"You may do it," breathed Saxon.

They stared up at their pillar with the avalanche of books around it. Saxon patted the pillar.

"It will not fall," she said.

"Can we go?"

They trotted through the underworld. The stone stairs chilled their feet. They pulled open the door to EGYPTOLOGY.

"Everything is brown," whispered Gilbert.

Saxon pushed her fingertips through dust on the door.

Her toes curled into grit. She slid her foot and it skidded dangerously. She showed Gilbert.

"Wait," said Saxon, and left him.

In a hundred heartbeats she returned with the tin of biscuits, and held them as if in offering; but not to Gilbert. "I promised bread to the Brogan, but WED will soon be gone."

Gilbert nodded, then with every care, they crossed ARMS AND ARMOUR to the stairs.

Saxon kept her promise as far as she could, by taking the biscuits – how she wished they were bread! – to the balcony.

She placed the tin on the tiles. She brushed dust with her palm; it was finer here, as if the grit could not drift as high; and the tiles were prettier than in her world, smaller, pink and blue as well as black and white. And she saw, a span away, scuffs in the dust.

She saw knuckle marks. And ugly trails, like dragging feet; and narrow lines, but she could not think what made the lines.

The balcony spread above ARMS AND ARMOUR. A corridor sped through archways, its walls glowing with flat glass cases Saxon could not see into; and heads, some white, like the last victim for brushing; and whole figures, seemingly about to move.

Something moved.

Rattling from behind a pillar; hair flowing, hands thrusting at the floor –

The Brogan –

Saxon leapt back, spear up to pierce the rags; but dust betrayed her, slipping underfoot, and she thudded on to the round edges of steps, rolling, bone against stone, the dagger bruising her thigh, spear clattering, tangling her legs, snapping! oh, not breaking! stunned she fell, sprawled on the landing; Homer in bronze, silent on his lyre.

But dust betrayed the Brogan too, and Saxon, dazed, saw it jab with its hands to stop. It juddered sideways, then swept against the biscuit tin. It toppled, rolling horribly fast, biscuits flying, the Brogan crashing beside Saxon, plunging across her legs – and breaking in two.

Horror turned the world dark for Saxon. Something dragged her. The Brogan's hair slid like a thousand threads on her feet. She screamed, and found Gilbert pulling her. She ran in his grasp through ARMS AND ARMOUR, over the boxes into EGYPTOLOGY, gasping when pain in her back knocked her to her knees; then into THE COFFEE SHOP.

"What must I do?" cried Gilbert.

"Cold water," moaned Saxon.

Gilbert brought a red basin wobbling with water.

Saxon eased her arms into it. "Unstrap my dagger. And please bring a cloth." He brought a cloth, and she removed her sealskin trousers. She held the healing coldness against her thigh.

"You must do my back," she said. Gilbert pushed up her jacket and she gasped at the shock of water.

Saxon explored bruises on her shins and remembered with dismay, her broken spear. She remembered the Brogan, also broken.

"What is it?" she sighed. "How could it break? Did you see? Did you see?"

"I saw, Saxon. But I didn't look. I snatched you away. For ten heartbeats I thought you were dead. Are your bruises cold?"

"Thank you, Gilbert. You may make my coffee."

"I will make food."

"You must clean. The dust – "

"I will clean," said Gilbert. "We will get another spear. Tomorrow."

"No! Today!"

"It is too late," said Gilbert. "We have never used spears in sleeptime. Tomorrow. We will eat before darkness. I will bring paper towels to dry your bruises."

So Saxon dabbed at her back; she pressed towels to her legs and arms. She replaced the dagger on her thigh, regretting her spear, wondering at the brushing to come. CENTRAL HALL stood veiled in brown.

She wiped a table with the cloth, wincing as her back alarmed her with pain, but she wiped widely, walking round the table, polishing the surface with water.

She cleaned another table, making her muscles work, stretching occasionally to her full slim height, bending her knees to be certain she would not break.

Then she cleaned the other four tables and busily rubbed the chairs; then Gilbert said "Ready," and the smell of steak made her mouth wet. They ate tinned steak and boiled potatoes, with only a little grit on the plates.

"I should have brushed the floor first," said Saxon, thinking of her clean tables and chairs. "The dust will rise."

"We will put one table top-down on another,"

mumbled Gilbert.

"Correct thinking, Gilbert! And we will stack the chairs. You have cleaned well in the kitchen."

"I cleaned while the potatoes boiled."

"The potatoes are good without salt," said Saxon, and Gilbert groaned, and they laughed, their laughter fluttering, it seemed, around the columns of stone.

The fluttering swept close and perched on the rail, tilting a bright glance at the food.

Another sparrow landed. And more.

"I will leave the potatoes," Saxon told the birds. "We are glad you survived the dust!" Then something changed.

The sparrows surged uneasily.

The world darkened.

"The lights are going out," said Gilbert.

They finished their meal as the chandeliers in CENTRAL HALL switched off, row by row. Night lights glowed in archways; the great doors shone dull; and the clock's green message hung in gloom.

THE COFFEE SHOP lights stayed lit, making the table-top space into a bright cage.

The children walked around the cold strength of pillars, into SHOP, where magazines, and things with no purpose lay importantly under a single spotlight. They fingered dust-brown books; they used SHOP's toilet, then rolled on to shelves softened with clothes from a rail.

Saxon shut her eyes.

She sighed towards sleep. But bruises tightened

43

her skin and her right hand was naked without her spear. She drew the dagger.

She straightened her back.

This had been a bad WED.

From the darkness of the shelf above, the Brogan tumbled on to her and broke. Spiders crowded around, not touching her, but shuffling. Could anything live after breaking? She stared up; there was no darkness – only shadows beyond SHOP's spotlight; her dreams had fled.

She said, "Gilbert." But his breath whispered without speech. She smiled and let her eyes shut.

Perhaps, after all, WED had not been so bad.

THUR

Her cheek was sticky where she had dribbled. She rolled from the shelf, checking the floor for spiders, dagger dipped like a spear. She returned the dagger to its sheath.

Gilbert woke. "Goodmorning, Saxon. It is THUR."

"Goodmorning, Gilbert. It is THUR." They clasped each other, using their left arms.

In the kitchen, Gilbert cooked bacon and eggs while Saxon kneaded bread and placed it over a ventilator in the floor; warm air would make the dough rise. She covered the dough with a dishtowel.

They ate breakfast in THE COFFEE SHOP and Saxon smiled.

"You have had a correct thought," said Gilbert.

Saxon put bacon into her smile.

She chewed, and swallowed.

"Speak," he ordered.

"The dust – " Saxon leaned slightly towards CENTRAL HALL, " – is our friend."

Gilbert scooped egg on to his fork. "Our friend?"

"What d'you see on the rail?"

"Dust."

"Sparrows were on it."

"I see their claw marks."

"And are spiders' legs not as long as a sparrow's claws?"

Gilbert swallowed his egg. "Yes…"

"Then the dust," said Saxon, "will show us where the spiders have walked. And with FIRE EXTINGUISHER – "

"We can kill them all! Oh, correct thinking, Saxon! You may make my coffee! Coffee!"

And they made coffee, and washed their dishes and the dishes from the day before, Gilbert telling the sparrows there were no crumbs because there was no bread; then they brushed THE COFFEE SHOP's rubber floor and wiped the rails between the pillars.

"A spear," said Gilbert, when the brushes rested behind the silver cabinet.

"A spear," said Saxon, easing her muscles.

They strode over the rail – Saxon carefully because of her bruises – and advanced into CENTRAL HALL.

Dust rose thick between their toes. The orrery lay sunk in brown waves. The children waded. They guessed where cardboard traps blocked the floor beneath the arch into ETHNOGRAPHY, and stepped high.

They advanced with enormous caution among almost-forgotten pillars, and glass cases glowing behind brown veils. They ignored the threatening armour of a Samurai.

They stopped once, smiling at plastic Eskimos naked in a shattered case; Saxon and Gilbert were wearing their clothes.

At a corner where the dust spread thin, a bump attracted Gilbert's blade.

He touched the bump and it slid. He turned it, and legs popped free of the dust. He burst it instinctively. But the spider was already dead.

"Perhaps," he breathed, "the dust is more of a friend than we thought." Then they trod carefully around the corner and stared.

In a gallery before them, dust towered to the ceiling.

They gazed in wonder. Display cases leaned, as if God had turned in his sleep beneath the floor. Saxon saw stained glass. She pointed and said, "That great window has collapsed letting the dust in." And though she whispered, the brown mountain shuddered, and grit slid, puffing dust towards the children.

But they did not run. The mountain settled.

"There must be a way," breathed Saxon – grit shifted.

"What?"

" – to get outside."

Saxon suddenly knew she had said something terrible.

Gilbert's eyes struck blue at her face.

She pressed her lips tight.

Then he laughed in a whisper. "It is only dust and darkness." He faced the mountain. "That is not correct thinking."

"No."

But Saxon was not sure. "I must have a spear," she said.

"The spears are buried."

"It is an avalanche," replied Saxon. "Like the avalanche from the blue bird. It may only block the gallery – not fill it. Come."

She strode under an arch, and entered the gallery again, beyond the dust. She stood on the hem of the avalanche. Smiling.

Her dagger levered the door of a case. Empty hooks reminded Saxon of their first search for weapons; many weapons were displayed throughout the world, but only African spears were light enough.

She chose a spear and tested it by trying to break off the head. The point dug blunt on her thumb.

She hefted the spear to find its balance. It had no thong.

Terrible faces glared into the gallery from a case half buried; faces of wood, decorated with fronds of leather.

Saxon stepped high, dust to her thighs, levered the glass door, and broke thongs from a mask, Nigerian, early nineteenth century. The thongs were brittle. She tucked them into her belt; oil would soften them. She turned towards Gilbert. She took a step. Dust slid around her legs.

Something cold met the sole of her foot.

She snatched back, thrust! with the spear, and the spear skidded – not because it was blunt – but because the object was hard.

Her heart rattled horridly. She panted. Gilbert's spear poised, eyes startled, blue as Wedgwood in his porcelain face.

The memory of the object was printed on Saxon's foot.

It wasn't a spider.

She dug with her spear; metal touched glass. She fumbled in the dust shoulder-deep, and her fingers closed on –

A smile tightened over her teeth. She stood up, grit draining from her arm.

Gilbert relaxed.

"A bottle!" he breathed; and the mountain rustled.

Saxon let her smile close around her eyes. She would explain the meaning of the bottle while they ate.

Saxon lifted the dishtowel from the dough. "It's not ready. If you will make coffee, I will sharpen my spear."

She crouched by a column in THE COFFEE SHOP

48

and rubbed metal on stone, thinning the blade until its touch was death, spilling a tiny avalanche of grey dust; she grinned at the bottle so innocent on a table.

She remembered the thongs and went to the kitchen, pulling them carefully from her belt. She placed them in a baking tray and poured vegetable oil over them. One was thin; she dropped it into a bin bag: the girl's head was still to be disposed of.

Saxon walked to THE COFFEE SHOP and stared at the dust in CENTRAL HALL. Such a brushing. She lifted the bottle, holding it to her chest. Perhaps the brushing need never be done.

"Coffee!"

The bottle stood between them on the table, transparent, slightly green. They drank coffee poured from the silver pot, and smoked cigars.

Gilbert's hair lay brown with dust. Clean streaks on his face showed his pale skin. Saxon knew she looked similar; but taller. And taller than she had been. Only recently could she reach across the table. Gilbert would not wish to hear that. He did not like change.

She said, "Gilbert."

He raised his glance hard on her eyes. Saxon knew he sensed her mood.

"Speak," he ordered. Smoke willowed from his cigar.

"Outside – " Saxon was unsure how to tell her strange idea.

"Dust," said Gilbert.

"And a bottle," said Saxon quickly.

"What? How can a bottle be outside? There is only dust and darkness! There can be no bottle." Gilbert frowned into his coffee.

"It was in the dust. Oh, Gilbert! Don't you see! It came in with the avalanche! That means...!"

"Nothing! Nothing! We have found bottles like that in rubbish bins. It was toppled from a rubbish bin!"

Saxon's mouth stayed open. A rubbish bin. She shook her head. Tears warmed her eyes. Her beautiful idea, killed.

She sucked her cigar and jetted smoke, trying to enjoy it. Oh, well.

Gilbert was right.

"And it is forbidden," whispered Gilbert.

"Forbidden?" Saxon bent a smile at him, then stared.

Gilbert curled into his chair. His eyes widened, and his voice soared with fear. "It is forbidden!" he gasped.

"What do you mean? What do you mean! The balcony is forbidden because of the Brogan! Did I forbid outside?"

"No! No, no, no!"

He wept, and she ran to him around the table; but he sat straight and knuckled his eyes.

"I'm sorry, Saxon, I don't know what I meant. Please. We must think about real things. The spiders..."

"You are correct?"

Gilbert nodded.

"Then," said Saxon, wondering at Gilbert's outburst, "we will see if the Brogan lives. And we will see if the spiders die. But you must wash your face."

Gilbert washed in the kitchen. Saxon cut cheese. Gilbert clattered the dishes into the sink. He sang as Saxon piled raisins and figs on a tray.

They left THE COFFEE SHOP, following foot dents in the dust, pointing at the dimpled imprints of their toes; through EGYPTOLOGY: Saxon glancing into MINERALOGY, disturbed by the fossil tree stumps displayed at angles to the floor. Past gods. Past the mummy, and an archway into ARMS AND ARMOUR where the empty men stared from the gloom.

"The dust has darkened the world," sighed Gilbert.

They stepped over the traps, past the two dead spiders and, with vigilance, approached the stairs.

On the steps, dust and a few biscuits. Saxon ran up to the landing. The blue bird sagged towards her. Homer wore a brown pile hat. With her toe, she touched the broken haft of her spear. The killing end had gone.

"It has taken the biscuit tin," she whispered, "and, I think, most of the biscuits."

She strode up to the balcony.

"I have brought food!" she said.

"...food!" said the long corridor.

"I have put it on the top step!"

"... top step, step..."

"I'm sorry there is no bread, but the dust..."

"...dust, dust..."

She hated this mocking, but she stared along past the flat glowing cases.

Gilbert touched her elbow. "Come," he said.

Stone archways looped into the distance at one side of the corridor.

"It may be hurt," whispered Saxon.

"It has the spear."

"Listen."

Whispering, from beyond EGYPTOLOGY.

"It is the dust," said Saxon too loudly. "It trickles."

"…ickles, trickles…"

They ran down the stairs.

Across ARMS AND ARMOUR.

They stood at the cardboard traps under the arch to PALAEONTOLOGY. The glass eye of PTERANODON shone down on them. The monster hung from wires, its jaw gaping, frilled with teeth, its wings laden with brown dust.

Reluctantly, Saxon leaned her spear against a column. She lifted a black bottle from its hook. She followed Gilbert over the boxes, Saxon hugging the bottle, Gilbert's spear offering death. The trails of many spiders marked the dust.

Far away, beyond STEGOSAURUS Saxon glimpsed the unlit display case. It sat dark beneath the lights. Almost black. But monsters barred the way; too large to be contained by glass, rearing ceiling-high, dust in their armour; dust lumped on the floor, making everything wilder, more threatened by eyes and mighty limbs; Saxon less sure that the beak of TRICERATOPS did not dip in curiosity, less sure that the white bones of the giant BRONTOSAURUS did not twitch as she passed by.

They knelt on the base of STEGOSAURUS, and peered round a leathery leg, hiding, felt Saxon, from the black case. A crack cut a shadow across the tiles. Saxon guessed this was the spiders' entrance to the world below. She stood straight, clutching the cylinder, touching with her body, the creature's armoured bulk. She stared at the darkened display case.

Gilbert rose beside her.

He gasped, and she drew in a breath, suddenly understanding what she was seeing.

Spiders moved on a pile of boxes. They used the boxes as Saxon would use stairs, scuttling on to the display case, dropping inside, clinging on webs, masses of spiders crowding the glass, blocking the interior light, trembling in the warmth of the bulbs.

Saxon groaned. She turned away, shuddering. FIRE EXTINGUISHER slid from her arms and clanged between the STEGOSAURUS' legs. She ran, ignoring trails in the dust, trying not to see the glassy mass of eyes.

A spider plopped open at her toes; Gilbert's blade plopped into another spider; and Saxon's panic dissolved. They ran together towards the boxes beneath the arch.

They leapt into EGYPTOLOGY. Saxon snatched up her spear and turned. Around the base of STEGOSAURUS, the spiders flowed like black water.

"They will swamp the boxes!" gasped Gilbert.

Saxon ran to a pillar. She snatched down another bottle and rushed it into Gilbert's arms. "Rest your spear! Squeeze the handle!" She swung away as mist spurted, but Gilbert's cry made her reach for him. The bottle fell, his hand staying on the pipe, making him bend.

"It burns!"

Saxon glanced at the spiders. They spread across the gallery, flowing around displays.

She felt the bottle. "It is cold!" she protested.

Saxon stood the bottle on end.

"I can't let go!" Gilbert's fingers eased on the pipe which joined the horn to the cylinder.

"You must let go! They are coming!"

Gilbert jerked his breath. He peeled his fingers free.

"Your skin is on the metal! Oh, hurry! The horn does not burn!"

Gilbert grasped the horn.

Saxon ran to another archway. Then together, they marched on the spiders, breathing death.

Blasting up dust.

Matchstick legs flying.

Bodies sliding and rolling, piling into ridges like plums spilled from many tins.

Gilbert's bottle ceased. Saxon swept a path to an archway where another cylinder waited.

Then they closed on the glass case, spraying it, the glass suddenly white, bang! dropping in shards, gas freezing the interior, webs frosted into lace, bulbs exploding; Saxon crinkled her cheek.

They took time to finish. Spiders scuttled on the boxes. Saxon noticed a gap in the wooden top of the case, wide enough for a spiders' archway.

They threw the boxes aside.

The crack in the floor wandered up the gallery

wall. Dust stood out of the crack; not loose dust, but glistening, as if mixed with saliva; and spider-size holes stared out. They thrust the horns at the holes, squeezing the handles until the cylinders ceased.

Then they staggered, suddenly exhausted; dropping the cylinders; Saxon's bruises aching, Gilbert nursing his wounded fingers.

"There's blood on your cheek," he said.

They went to the toilet behind SHOP. Because the toilet had a drain in the floor, they stripped off their clothes, shook them, beat them fiercely with

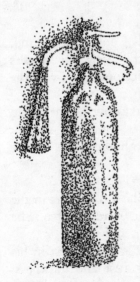

the spears, then washed each other by pouring water from a bucket over their heads. Spiders' legs gathered in the drain. They dried themselves, and Saxon abandoned the seal-skins and chose shirts and skirts from a rail in SHOP; but they ripped the skirts and fastened the daggers to their thighs. Then they returned to THE COFFEE SHOP. Saxon put pink oint-ment on Gilbert's fingers.

She let him choose a book from the case on the counter; and with much straightening of her bruised back, she put bread in the oven, chipped potatoes, and prepared cherry cake.

She sat alone in the kitchen while the bread baked; breathing its smell, thinking of the fossil tree stumps. She wondered at their shape – not measured into straight lines and perfect curves like the world, but – she smiled – like Gilbert, and the sparrows. And the spiders.

How strange that she could divide creation in two: that which is measured, and that which is not.

She took the bread from the oven, turned down the heat and put in the cake.

"Cold meat and chips," she announced, and Gilbert thanked her from behind his book. He ate.

"You are thoughtful," said Saxon.

"There are so many words I don't understand. What is *rain*? And *sky*? And *miles*?" His fingers spread limp on an open dictionary. "Even the meaning has no meaning."

"There is much we don't know," murmured Saxon.

"The spiders came through the holes in the dust," whispered Gilbert.

"Yes."

Saxon finished her food. She left Gilbert in the muddle of his thoughts and made coffee. She served the cake which was hot and soft.

"They came from outside?" said Gilbert in his tiniest voice. "There is only dust and darkness. We know that."

"We believe that." Saxon bit her cake, catching crumbs on her palm.

"But if they did come from outside, then..."

Saxon dabbed up crumbs on her tongue.

"…there could be other things." He looked at the bottle.

"Sparrows?" suggested Saxon.

"No. Sparrows could not fly in the dust. I don't know."

"Don't you want to find out? Eat your cake."

Gilbert angled the cake into his mouth. He seemed not to hear her question. He finished the cake and licked his hands.

"There is much brushing to be done." He stared over the rail into CENTRAL HALL.

"Afterwards," said Saxon gently. "After we go outside."

Gilbert's eyes swung at her, blue, and large with dismay.

"We must!" she urged. "We must try! Try!"

"We cannot live in dust!" he shrieked.

"Neither can spiders! Did we not find them buried and dead in the great avalanche? Yet they tunnel in the dust! They survive!"

"What purpose! Shall we tunnel for ever? The dust has no end – "

"How do you know!"

Gilbert's glance jerked away. She heard his throat move.

"It has no end," he whimpered. Blue veins beat in his temple. Then he turned on Saxon. "What else could there be?"

"Another world!" hissed Saxon. "Perhaps a better world. Without spiders. Without the Brogan!"

She added a new thought. "What," she said,

"if the world groans again? What if the windows fall, and the pillars tremble until they break?"

A crumb sat on Gilbert's lip. His tongue came out and licked it inside.

" – what a mighty brushing that would be."

Gilbert wept.

He strode towards SHOP.

Saxon drank coffee. She chose a cigar, touched it on her lips, returned it to the box. She cleared the table, leaving cake crumbs. She tapped the table with her fingernails. Sparrows dropped from above the chandeliers and huddled on the rail.

"Eat," said Saxon. She stepped among the sparrows, spear level, into CENTRAL HALL. The clock said 14.47 THUR. 4 YEARS 82 DAYS FROM HOSTILITIES.

She took a brush from behind the silver cabinet. Above chirrupings she said, "I am brushing," but no answer came from SHOP.

She brushed casually, to please Gilbert. She pushed a clean circle around the AMMUNITION box, and wandered, leaving a dizzy trail, amusing herself rather than working.

Near the orrery the brush stuck in deep dust and Saxon sneezed. She sneezed! dropping the brush, stepping away.

Towards the great doors.

Dust on every wooden ridge.

Dust on every square of glass.

She waded calf-deep and rubbed a pane clean; she saw her reflection, and a glimmer of grit pressed on the other side.

She fingered the door handle; curved like the coffee pot handle but large, and the metal yellow, not the dull grey of silver.

Her fingers tightened around it. Her heart throbbed as if she had met spiders.

She pulled open one great door.

Dust sprinkled on her head.

Grit tumbled in around her feet.

It filled the doorway. It sparkled in the light of the chandeliers. Saxon smiled rather grimly. Dust and darkness. But she thrust suddenly with her spear and grit slid to embrace her hips. She sneezed; and took tiny steps, building dust under her feet. She fell backwards, oh! sneezing! and rolled free.

Gasping.

Wondering if Gilbert was right.

But now one of the great doors stood open.

On the outside of the door Saxon saw a word in faded gold letters. "Entrance," she read.

"Saxon!"

Gilbert running on the soft floor. "You cannot!"

He stared at her legs and hair, her dust-brown arms. "You must not!" he gasped.

"Must not? Must not? Is it fear that speaks, Gilbert? Is it fear?" Her voice soared. "Outside–"

She knotted her fingers into the arm of his clean shirt. "Outside is darkness and dust! And spiders! And maybe a bottle!" She released him. "If the bottle did come from outside, then God is outside. Would He then, create dust that goes on for ever, with just one bottle? Oh, Gilbert! there may be another world! It may be a hundred paces away. It may be a single span." She took his wrists and spread his arms to show how near the new world might be. "We must try, Gilbert, you and I."

Tears folded out of Gilbert's eyes. He caught them on his left sleeve. She welcomed him into her embrace.

In the wall of grit where her spear had pierced, was the beginning of a tunnel.

Excitement blazed a smile across Saxon's face.

She strode to the silver cabinet and dashed her spear-haft through the glass.

"Saxon!" They had learned long ago that anything broken was never replaced.

From the display Saxon snatched a scoop, silver, eighteenth century, English; large enough to hold a small loaf. She ran to the AMMUNITION box and lifted the shovel from the sugary heap of the girl's head.

She threw it at Gilbert and he caught its handle. She dug. Gilbert stood behind her, casting shadows.

Saxon worked without speaking.

The shovel scraped and Gilbert's shadows departed as he carried grit out of Saxon's way. Then he crowded her shoulder, and together they opened the tunnel's mouth.

They sweated. Dust stuck to their faces, turned their clean clothes brown.

The tunnel's sides enclosed them. Saxon grinned at Gilbert and he smiled. She did not say, "We are outside."

The tiled floor of CENTRAL HALL became stone beyond the door. Saxon dug deep with the scoop; she dug deeper than the stone floor.

She sat back, her hair against the tunnel's roof.

"A step!" whispered Gilbert.

They burrowed furiously, until dust choked them, making them crawl away to stand by the orrery, breathing; Gilbert's eyes gleaming.

Then they stroked swiftly, but with less dust rising, and uncovered another step.

At the fourth step they cut the roof higher and carried debris into CENTRAL HALL.

Then they crawled into the gloom of their diggings, and Gilbert uncovered a stone.

It lay broken on the steps.

A shiver trembled Saxon's back. She rubbed grit from her lips.

"It's only a stone," said Gilbert.

"A long time ago – " whispered Saxon, and Gilbert looked at her swiftly, " – something happened. Right here."

"But we are outside," protested Gilbert.

"Yes," said Saxon.

Then they worked, but she let Gilbert dig around the stone.

They found a shoe.

In the darkness of the tunnel it was difficult to see.

"We must rest anyway," said Saxon, so they emerged into CENTRAL HALL.

They were astonished at the green numbers on the clock.

"It will soon be sleeptime," said Gilbert.

"Put the shoe in THE COFFEE SHOP," ordered Saxon. "We must wash again."

They took more fresh clothes from SHOP, then with much stretching of muscles, they went to the kitchen, Gilbert dabbing his fingers thick and pink with ointment, Saxon trying to decide between roast beef and bacon, then choosing bacon because of the tasty picture on the tin.

So they ate bacon and chips, with peas from the freezer which were greener than canned peas, and rolled better around their plates.

The shoe lay on the table with the bottle, its faint red skin shining in the glass. Between bites Saxon tried it on.

"It fits my right foot better," she said. "But it squeezes my toes."

"I don't think God made it for you," smiled Gilbert.

Saxon grinned. "No. He made it for..."

Her smile slackened. She put a chip on her tongue.

A thought had crept to the edge of her mind.

"Do you think," she murmured, "it was made to be worn?"

"No!" cried Gilbert laughing. "Ha! Were the Victorian shoes? Or the armour!"

"Oh, I know!" said Saxon. "But..."

The shoe was cracked; she turned it over and rubbed the rough underside with her thumb. Inside, traces of words were unreadable.

"Gilbert?"

"Mmm?"

"What if it was made for..." Her thought demanded words she did not have. "Not you..."

"Correct thinking."

"...and not me."

"Yes."

"Another."

"What do you mean? The bacon was a good choice, Saxon."

"Thank you, Gilbert. It is very good."

She pushed the shoe at Gilbert.

"Do you not think," she breathed excitedly, "that it seems used?"

Gilbert leaned back, the Picasso poster softly coloured behind his head; he broke chips with his fork for the sparrows. "I don't know what you mean."

"Look at it, Gilbert!" she hissed.

"I am looking."

"Look at the underneath. Is it not rubbed like the inside of your spear sleeve?"

"It's the way God made it," mumbled Gilbert.

"Is it? Why would he make it worn? Would he not make it perfect like the glass cases and the stone columns?"

"But most things are not perfect. Some animals are split, and their insides crumble. Lights in EXHIBITION GALLERY will not switch on. It's the way things are."

Saxon forked up the last of her bacon and peas. "There is cake," she said. "I will make coffee. Sit."

She worked in the kitchen, her mind solemn with the idea of Another. In her memory she examined dummies in dresses stained as if with sweat; or worn as if used. But Saxon had never used them. Nor Gilbert.

Was Another in the world? She remembered the shoe; or outside the world?

She carried the cherry cake and the silver coffee pot on a tray. Gilbert was gazing at the shoe, not touching it.

"On the door," whispered Saxon, and Gilbert jumped as she placed the tray at his elbow, "is the word ENTRANCE. Why, Gilbert, did God build the most beautiful doors in the world with ENTRANCE on the outside?"

Saxon knew her question had no answer, but she sat and poured coffee, and waited.

Gilbert's face closed around his feelings, shutting her out. He cut the cake. He shrugged, his face opening into a smile. He pushed the cake towards her. Saxon realized how tired he was.

"I wonder if the Brogan has eaten," she said.

"We should have fed it again. It will throw another head."

Saxon gazed at the dust in CENTRAL HALL. "We should have brushed," she said, "and hunted the last of the spiders."

"And remembered our other name."

Saxon turned to the shoe. Tears moved in her eyes. "I don't know."

Then they sat until sleep urged them to bed.

And to sigh; and to ignore the darkening lights, pretending they heard no weeping deep in the corridors above the world.

Perhaps it was a dream; a dream which

lingered long into sleeptime. Sleeptime.

FRI

Saxon toasted slices of new bread. She served breakfast among the columns of THE COFFEE SHOP, where Gilbert stretched his wounded fingers and prodded them into ointment.

"Is your sealskin correct?" asked Saxon.

"Correct, thank you, Saxon," said Gilbert, but he wriggled, and Saxon smiled for her sealskin too, scratched grittily.

"We will take cheese to the Brogan," said Saxon, "and bread. I don't remember," she murmured, "how I learned to make bread."

"You have strange ideas, Saxon."

"But isn't it strange that we know things, yet can't remember how we know?"

"We have always known," shrugged Gilbert. "But – " He sighed over his warm roll and marmalade. " – what caused the trembling, Saxon?"

"Oh." Saxon glanced into CENTRAL HALL where their feet had flattened a path to the tunnel. "God sneezing," she murmured.

Gilbert smiled.

They jogged along EGYPTOLOGY, a plastic bag of food bouncing on Saxon's hip. She stared into

ARMS AND ARMOUR, where hollow bodies startled her.

In MINERALOGY the slanted tables glowed faintly. Nothing stirred, except Saxon's memory as she glimpsed the fossil tree stumps poised at angles to the floor.

Dust rustled on light bulbs. Ancient gods wore new brown dresses; and the air tasted – not of dust – but...

"Can you smell something?" asked Gilbert.

Saxon's face crinkled as the smell attacked her nostrils.

They peered into PALAEONTOLOGY, mouths tight, glancing at each other in astonishment, for the mounds of spiders shone, like certain minerals in MINERALOGY.

Saxon hurried Gilbert into ARMS AND ARMOUR and on to the stairs. Glass from the blue bird cracked under their feet. Saxon gazed at the empty stone window-frame, for grit had vomited in, burying Homer, leaving exposed only one bronze knee.

On the balcony the tray they had left earlier now held crumbs, hammered fine by sparrows.

"The Brogan has not eaten," whispered Saxon, and the long corridor breathed her words, as if the heads spoke. And because she hated the Brogan, Saxon's mouth smiled, but fear crawled in her mind and she touched the bag of food; she pointed down the corridor.

Gilbert's lips shaped a red NO! but Saxon pointed again, and he dashed into a head's shadow.

His finger flashed and Saxon hid with him. Through an archway she saw many paintings, each lit by its own electric glow.

Gilbert ran to the archway, signalled, and vanished.

Saxon's feet padded on small tiles. In the gallery, soft red benches waited as if God had known she and Gilbert would come. Beyond another arch, Gilbert waved. She trotted, astounded at the colours and images in the paintings. Had God created all this for her?

Gilbert stood before a cross, granite, Celtic, Inverurie; higher than a spear's reach.

Saxon faced the cross, and astonishment opened her mouth as her knee bent and her right hand leapt to her chest, moving on her chest without thought.

And Gilbert stared; and Saxon gaped at her hand. Then she walked among the paintings.

Colours knocked at the door of memory. Saxon clutched her head, her spear dangling on its thong, trying to hold memory shut.

Then she ran; thinking only of finding the Brogan. Feed it, do your duty to it, let it not be broken; how can it, how can it be broken and live? Feet speeding on tiles, on carpet, plastic rustling at her belt; she leapt on to a seat, heart fast; her mind sought a noise.

Gilbert strode beside her on to the soft red bench; she dipped her head, and he listened.

Air sighed in a vent.

A strip light buzzed.

Painted children played in silence.

Saxon heard her throat swallow.

Gush! struck her ear, distantly.

She held Gilbert's glance; he too, recognized the rush of a tap turned on.

They ran from the bench as silent as smoke from a dying cigar. Under an arch; on to a balcony heaped with shadow. Two children met them.

Saxon and Gilbert stopped in wonder. Two children, high on a plinth, a girl, smaller than Saxon, holding a tiny boy on her shoulder; both naked and beautiful, cold beneath Saxon's astonished fingers; the boy laughing, the girl smiling patiently, gazing down on Saxon, saying, "Understand me if you can. Is God not mysterious beyond comprehension, for am I not you a hundred days ago with my hair loose, and is this boy not Gilbert as memory holds him?"

Gilbert reached between the statue's feet, touching something with his left hand; little pieces of something, dark and furry. He held his fingers to his nose, and Saxon bent.

It was cheese.

Cheese she had given the Brogan. Here, between these beautiful feet, left to moulder before the children of bronze.

Given by the Brogan.

And sadness rose in Saxon. Sadness warmed with her tears. And anger at not understanding. She turned her anger on the Brogan, threatening – in her head – to throw the bag of food away, or leave it, perhaps, between those cold feet.

But she followed Gilbert. Then, on another

balcony, where spotlights split the darkness, a
door stood open laying a fan of light on the tiles;
and a sound placed greater anger on Saxon's
heart.

Why weeps the Brogan?

Saxon turned her back. She leaned on the
balustrade, spear tight in her fist, stone cool
under her knuckles. Below hung chandeliers dim
with dust; on one, a spot of paper, red as ketchup.
Saxon wondered who had thrown it. Then she
remembered only she and Gilbert were in the
worlds – and the Brogan. Another did not exist.

Gilbert touched her. She led him towards the
fan of light.

But the light was not theirs to step on, so they
stood with their toes in shadow, speartips bright,
as the weeping sank to moaning. Saxon untied
the food from her belt. Should she leave it? Or
call out? When the Brogan raged, it threw heads.

But it was broken.

She decided.

She waved Gilbert behind her and touched the
door with her blade. She twisted her glance on to
him. His eyes sat huge in his white face.

She pushed the door.

Wire writhed from a socket into an electric
heater; and a red bench sat with its back to the

door.

Saxon eased the door wide, revealing the room. A wall with soft green board on it, and pinned about the board, papers, faded and curled. An orange cup drained beside a metal sink. Rags dripped from a string.

Saxon held out the plastic bag.

She shook the bag.

The moaning ceased.

A drip from the rags echoed in the sink; silence filling with tension.

The spear-head lunged over the back of the bench, stabbing, horribly gripped in the Brogan's fingers, muscles in the slim arm flickering with effort, the top of the head glimpsed. Fury and frustration –

Saxon tossed the food over the bench.

The arm jerked out of sight.

The silence returned; but with a quality of astonishment, thought Saxon. Plastic rustled; and eating sounds.

Then: flesh on the floor; a foot, or thigh, thudding on carpet.

Saxon backed Gilbert on to the balcony.

Dragging on the carpet. The door moved.

A hand extended into the light.

Arms hauled the body. Hair puffed from the hidden face, and protruding from the hair – as if clenched in the mouth – the broken spear.

Saxon said, "Oh!" and reached for Gilbert. They backed around a column. "It *is* broken!" she gasped. "Where is the other half!"

Fear in her blood as the Brogan pulled on to

the balcony.

It stopped. It balanced carefully, one hand taking the spear from its mouth.

Gilbert's fingers touched Saxon's arm.

With the spear's broken end, the Brogan drew a curve in the dust.

The spear lifted. Another curve, wobbling, joining to itself, making a grotesque ring.

Whimpers of fury.

A third mark, and a fourth. The spear slipped, and the hand beat the tiles.

"It's trying to write!" moaned Saxon, and horror overcame her. She ran, tears blurring the lights. And she fled, moaning among galleries, wailing in corridors, striking her body on stands, sending something crashing –

She shut her mind to the past.

Fossil tree stumps.

A stone broken on the steps outside the world.

A red shoe.

Her mind darkened, and memory vanished as she fainted.

Beneath Saxon pressed the familiar shape of steps.

She wiped her eyes. Stairs curved down to a landing, with a light over a door, then down further out of sight. Her footprints marked the dust.

Above, the stairs wound into blackness.

"Saxon!" Gilbert, shrill and distant.

She screamed to guide him, and untangled the spear thong from her fingers. "Up the stairs!"

"Coming!" Gilbert's voice, squashed by the staircase wall. His face peered from below the curve of an iron banister. "You are correct?"

"Better." Saxon breathed sobs.

The step under her feet vibrated.

A crack slithered across the ceiling.

In the darkness above, glass crashed, and grit rushed down.

The world danced.

"Run!" she gasped.

Gilbert leapt to the landing. "Here, Saxon!" and he thrust open the door beneath the light. She stumbled on the trembling stair then jumped –

For half a heartbeat she glanced back into spilling dust, and a shiver of awe thrilled her spine, then she was through the door, and it slammed.

She glimpsed the room. A slit window of lead and glass, blackness beyond; before it, a sill, softly cob-webbed, dangling with insects; and the wall curved close; Saxon thought if Another had been there, the space would be too small.

Then the door shut, blinding her.

They coughed dust.

"Jacket off! Off!"

Saxon loosed her spear and stripped away her sealskin, packing it under the door. They used knees and fingers to stuff the jackets tight, Saxon praying God would not fail them.

A sound boomed across the world; Saxon thought of the great doors. Then the trembling ceased, but grit whispered long on the stairs.

"Is it over?" Gilbert leaned close.

"Do not weep," gasped Saxon.

"I'm not."

"We must wait until the dust settles." She shut her mind against the avalanches that awaited brushing now.

"Our tunnel will have fallen," whispered Gilbert.

"Oh. Yes."

Saxon panted.

"We shall dig again," whispered Gilbert.

"Gilbert – "

"We must, Saxon. You were right. If more trembling comes we will need your other world – "

"Yes." Excitement shivered through her. "I saw a light!"

"A light? What d'you mean?"

"I looked up. Into the darkness on the stairs. As dark as this!" Her fingers found his face, and she wiped his tears. "Through the dust, Gilbert! Suddenly! A light! Oh, a most beautiful light! A light from God! – oh, Gilbert!" Her tears of joy overflowed.

" – the light was outside!"

Glass creaked in its lead strips.

Gilbert's hand fumbled into Saxon's palm.

"Outside?"

She nodded, then said, "Yes," in a voice that

hardly disturbed the air.

"Outside?"

She opened his hand and pressed it to her cheek.

"I don't understand." Gilbert's breath warmed her eyes. "Darkness and dust. A light?"

"A beautiful light! There is no light in the world like it! Oh, Gilbert!"

And she sat silent, for words did not exist for the hope that blossomed in her mind.

Deep in the world a great moan arose then died. Silence dropped around the children, and the weight of darkness pressed them into sleep.

Saxon woke, shivering. She felt her way into her jacket, nudging Gilbert.

"There are no vents in here. Put this on."

She pulled the door open. Grit fell on to her feet. Dusty light showed the edges of steps. "Come."

Dust buried her feet as she went up, prodding with the spear for balance.

"There may be glass," warned Gilbert.

She stared into the darkness.

"Can you see the light?"

"No."

She went up, holding the iron rail, probing the darkness with her spear. Grit rushed on her and she fled to the landing; the grit quietened, but dust chased them down the stairs to a gallery.

"Did you see the light?"

"We shall return. To dig. The staircase is blocked. Come. This is where our tunnel must be."

She hesitated, looking back through an arch to the staircase. She wondered how many worlds stood one upon another, for the light was higher than she had ever imagined.

"We must eat," said Gilbert, and they wandered, seeking the stairs to ARMS AND ARMOUR. But dust blocked many archways, and pillars leaned as if weary of supporting stone and plaster. And walls, dark with cracks, groaned foggily, sending them scuttling.

They walked on to a balcony, and stared into the gallery below. Saxon's fingers tightened on the fur-browned balustrade. The wreckage of glass cases sprawled desperately, and animals, stiff and undismayed, stood pop-headed out of dust piles, or reached free a hoof or rump to the misty air.

"This is not ARMS AND ARMOUR," whispered Gilbert.

Above the far side of the balcony, beyond the silent animals, a window splintered, and grit plunged in, as mad as water falling from a bucket; a light swung in the rush of air; the grit struck the balcony and spewed dust into the gallery below. Through the dust, behind the little pillars of the distant balustrade, something white shone at Saxon.

"We must find ARMS AND ARMOUR," said Gilbert. "I want to look..."

Saxon walked past cases displaying strange objects.

"What's a violin?" said Gilbert behind her.

She trotted.

"Saxon."

Round the balcony, avoiding a huge painting shaken from the wall and pierced by the arms of stone wrestlers.

"Saxon!"

The rush of grit from the window ceased.

Saxon walked closer, trying not to breathe dust.

A cough surprised her throat, and she stopped.

She blinked her eyes clean, leaning forward, trying to see...

Her heart beat hard, and gasps fled from her mouth.

She raised the spear, then put her hand on the balustrade to keep from falling. She turned, sweeping Gilbert back.

"What is it? Saxon! You'll knock me over!"

She ran until he stopped her, wrapping her in his arms and pulling her against a pillar. She huddled into him, shuddering.

"Tell me, Saxon! Tell me!"

"Oh, Gilbert!"

She pointed with her left hand.

Gilbert turned.

Excitement rose through Saxon's fear.

She shrieked at Gilbert. "It is Another!"

"Come," said Gilbert.

Memories boiled in Saxon.

"We must look." He took her pointing hand, and she followed.

She stared at the violin; piccolo, double bass.

Gilbert pulled her on.

She would be brave.

They approached, and crouched, wondering at the silver bulk beneath the dust.

Saxon stared at the roundness of the limbs.

"It is strange armour," she whispered.

They found the face, peaceful behind a window in the suit's head.

"Is it asleep?" asked Gilbert.

"The suit is puffed up," said Saxon, "like a plastic bag full of breath."

"Should we waken it?"

Saxon prodded the suit with her spear.

The point pierced the fabric. The suit hissed and collapsed. The eyelids flattened, as if the eyes had dropped inside the head; the children jumped back, spitting stench from their mouths.

Then they retreated, bewildered, wandering through the upper world, until Gilbert pointed to the red tray partly buried in dust.

They crept down to the gloom of ARMS AND ARMOUR. Iron men had toppled from their prisons, shattering the glass walls, scattering their metal bodies. Saxon thought of the Brogan in two pieces on the stairs.

"The dust is very deep!" gasped Gilbert.

"Yes." Saxon shut Another from her mind. "We must check the food store." She stepped high, prodding the dust with her spear for balance. They struggled under the arch into EGYP-

TOLOGY, striding over the buried spider traps. Grit rose in a mighty sweep, through the opposite arch, filling PALAEONTOLOGY, presenting a sloping wall to the children's astonished gaze; from the wall protruded the dreadful, helpless head of PTERANODON.

They went in fear, through PRIVATE, STAFF ONLY.

Dust softened the stone steps.

They hurried among the shelves of books; through the smell of rotting spiders. Saxon fled to the food store, dancing insanely over glowing heaps of her dead enemies. Gasping as plaster on the carpet jabbed her soles; ducking under steam gushing down from the anacondas; but she didn't think. She ran to the metal door. The illuminated sign was dark. She pushed the door and it swung silently. "The siren has failed!" She turned, looking for Gilbert.

He appeared in the distance, round the pillar where they had built the column of books at the other side of the shelves. He ran at her, staring into her face.

"The crack the spiders came through!" He spread his arms. "It is wide enough for Another! The books have fallen! Look! Look!" He nodded desperately at the ceiling, and Saxon saw why her feet had found plaster, and why steam spat on her. The pipes dangled, steam fizzing from splits and, in the ceiling, a great gash hung with rubble.

She gasped. "That could come down! The way to the food would be blocked! Hurry! Hurry!" And she dragged Gilbert into the store. Emergency bulbs glowed among dead strip lights.

"Check the temperature!"

Saxon ran to the freezer. Its padded wall breathed mist from a split big enough to walk through. A puddle crept across the floor.

"The temperature is up!" trilled Gilbert.

Saxon stared at the gauge on the freezer door. "This one's up too." She turned the wheel on the door and pulled. Plastic sacks hung in rows, their frosty jackets patched-dark with wet.

"Get a trolley!"

"What shall we do!"

"Move the food. Put it in PRIVATE, STAFF ONLY. We must get out of here quickly before that ceiling falls! All the dust in PALAEONTOLOGY will come down! The way will be blocked for ever! Hurry! Load the trolley! Tinned meats! Flour! Coffee, honey! Quickly! Butter and oil! And dried fruit! Move! Move!" Then they ran, heaving the trolley through the decaying glow of spiders, to the stone stairs.

The wheels bumped on the bottom step. "It's too heavy to carry up!" gasped Gilbert.

"Help me!" ordered Saxon, and they hung their weight on the trolley's side until it toppled. They leapt back from an avalanche of tins and packets. "Leave it! Run!" And they ran under the creaking ceiling, to the store.

How they worked. Sweat rolled on their skin. They kicked aside squelching spiders. They cringed under blasts of steam. Saxon's shoulders burned with strain. Her legs trembled until she could scarcely walk. And she glanced at Gilbert, and approved of his gasping silence, for sweat dripped from his chin, and the bones of his hands shone through his skin.

"We must rest!" said Saxon, and Gilbert sprawled on the steps, stripping off his jacket.

"The steps are cool!" he panted.

"The food should be safe here. Come." And he followed her, carrying his spear and jacket.

They walked through dust, avoiding the glare of PTERANODON, among the gods of EGYPTOLOGY. Saxon lifted a sparrow from the lap of Anubis, and Gilbert turned away. The sparrow was dead.

The mummy slept in darkness. The back of the bench stuck up out of the dust. They stumbled toward the sarcophagus, and leaned on its cool granite shoulders.

Gilbert's spear dropped from his hand. Saxon sank to her knees on the dust-soft floor. She breathed brown air.

In CENTRAL HALL they gazed on the golden pipes of the organ, leaning from the balcony. The balcony sagged, its little columns ready to fall; and the great doors of glass and wood stood at strange angles, torn from their doorways in a thrust of grit and dust which had come in from outside. The orrery was buried. A chandelier lay on the floor, and the children crawled to it and sat astounded at its great size. Heads lay, cushioned in their fall from the balcony, by God's brown carpet. The AMMUNITION box was somewhere under the carpet.

Stunned, Saxon led Gilbert to THE COFFEE SHOP. They strode shin-deep in the kitchen. In anger, Saxon hauled armfuls of dust from her worktops, threw platefuls of dust out of her sink. The green numbers on the clock changed many times before they ate; and no sparrows flew.

Then the heart went out of them, and they slept.

SAT

"Goodmorning, Gilbert," whispered Saxon. "It is SAT."

"Goodmorning, Saxon. It is SAT."

They embraced. Saxon rubbed Gilbert's shoulder. "You are very dirty."

"You are not very clean."

They washed, pouring water from the bucket over each other in the toilet. They beat their sealskins with the spears, then ate in the kitchen, glad again, as they were last night, that the cooker rings grew red; hot beans and bread. They gulped coffee. Gilbert opened the tin of plums. Saxon rattled a plate for the sparrows, and a few chittered down nervously.

"We must bring the food here," said Gilbert.

"Yes."

"In case the ceiling falls in the underworld."

Saxon's mind sat dull. She watched her hands prepare more coffee. She sliced bread, buttered it, fried bacon, squashed the bacon between slices. She filled a bottle with cooled coffee, and cut cheese.

"What are you doing?"

She poured raisins and figs into plastic bags.

"Is it for the Brogan? There is too much – "

"It is for the three of us." She stared at Gilbert, disturbed at her own words.

"But we must bring food here!"

"No," whispered Saxon.

"We must – "

"No." She shook her head, rustling her pigtail. "How many tins shall we bring, Gilbert? Enough to fill THE COFFEE SHOP? Should we pack CENTRAL HALL?"

"Please!"

"Gilbert, Gilbert, even if there isn't another trembling, are you content to live in the dust? content to spend forever learning the names of things in glass cases? Do you simply want to be safe?" She touched his cheek. "We must follow the light."

"Why can't we be safe and follow the light?"

"Because – " She held his hand and led him around the tables in THE COFFEE SHOP. She looked up at the organ pipes and the twisted balcony. She hadn't meant to tell him. "If there is another trembling," she said firmly, "that balcony may fall. Everything behind it will come down. Dust could fill CENTRAL HALL, perhaps as high as the chandeliers. THE COFFEE SHOP would be buried. If we were asleep, we would be buried." She tightened her grip on his fingers. "What" – she whispered, " – if all the lights went out?"

Gilbert's face collapsed with horror. Saxon

82

knelt, holding him. "I'm sorry!" she gasped. "I didn't mean it! I didn't!"

"But it's true!" sobbed Gilbert. "It could happen! Oh, Saxon what can we do!"

"It won't happen! God wouldn't allow it. Come. Dry your face. There. I have already begun. I have prepared the food."

"You want to dig for the light?"

"Yes."

"Past the Brogan?"

"We must feed the Brogan."

"How can the Brogan write?"

"I don't know."

"You really saw a light?"

"Yes."

"Outside?"

"Outside."

"I wish the sparrows could be safe."

Saxon tied the plastic bags to her belt. They rustled at her hips.

Gilbert stood in a little pit his feet had rubbed in the dust. Saxon saw that his dagger hung correctly; spear tall, glittering in THE COFFEE SHOP's lights; the coffee bottle firm in his left hand.

Slowly, Saxon looked around her kitchen. Tears waited release, but she breathed firmly. She touched her dagger; grasped her spear. She stuck the spear haft in the dust and strode to the storage jars; she threw aside lids, and emptied raisins, figs, sultanas, rice, lentils, barley.... She tapped a jar against the worktop and walked quickly with Gilbert – lifting the scoop from the counter – not glancing through THE COFFEE SHOP, striding high, beneath the arch into EGYPTOLOGY.

She avoided the stony gaze of Set and Anubis. She marched under the nearest arch into ARMS AND ARMOUR.

Her reflection stepped toward her in the dusty glass of a long display case. Her dagger struck at the lock. Gilbert helped slide the glass. She leaned her spear and lifted out a spetum. She bumped its haft on the floor and gazed up at the blade; such a blade – as long as Gilbert's arm, with two barbs curving back as big as plates: with such a blade on such a haft, they could reach up the stairs into the grit that hid the light.

The spetum was very heavy. Saxon couldn't carry everything. She needed the scoop. She lifted her spear and placed it in the cabinet. Gilbert touched her hand. She forced her lips to smile. Then she toppled the spetum on to her shoulder and waded towards the stairs that would take them into the world of the Brogan.

Gilbert flitted through shadows of the upper world, little puffs of dust bursting from his heels; Saxon wished she could clean the dust from the colours of the paintings. She walked, the spetum grinding her shoulder. Gilbert waited on the Brogan's balcony. Many bulbs stared, glassily dark.

In the gallery below, chandeliers hung lifeless amid hazy paths cut by spotlights.

The Brogan's door was shut.

Saxon pushed the scoop under Gilbert's arm.

Using both hands, she lowered the butt of the spetum to the tiles.

Heads watched.

Gilbert helped her lie the spetum in the dust.

Saxon pulled her dagger. She took the coffee bottle from Gilbert and walked towards the door. She stared at the Brogan's squiggles, partly filled-in since the second trembling.

Her heart throbbed, sickening her, as she unravelled the writing. The first letter was C; the wobbling ring, an O; F and F again. She shook the coffee bottle, but she did not know where her rage came from. But her memory of what the Brogan had written, was correct.

She marched to the door and knocked as if the Brogan were a person. She breathed firmly.

She panted. In her imagination a stone fell on the steps outside the great door. She shut her eyes, and saw the red shoe on THE COFFEE SHOP table. She knocked vigorously; then clicked the handle and pushed, letting out yellow light.

The socket swallowed the flex. The red bench was a hiding place. On the notice board, the papers hung scored and ripped.

"I have brought food!" gasped Saxon. "Coffee!"

The silence stood empty.

Saxon darted a glance over the bench. An open door showed a toilet. She hadn't thought that the Brogan...

She walked round the bench to the sink and left bags of food on the drainer. She poured coffee into the orange plastic cup. Pages from the notice board lay thrown in the sink. Ink bled from two halves of a pen. She saw COFFEE carved on several sheets; a printed notice, savagely crumpled, had different letters cut into it. She smoothed it –

"Saxon!"

Gilbert, at the door, beckoning.

Saxon ran round the bench, out among heads, cringing at the rustling plastic on her hips.

She held Gilbert in a pillar's shadow.

Her shoulder felt weightless. She touched Gilbert, and he looked. She groaned without sound. She had forgotten the spetum.

Gilbert's eyes closed, then he smiled, softening Saxon's dismay, and she loved him more fondly than ever.

Then they watched, waiting, for it was too late to go back.

The Brogan rushed into the doorway's yellow glow. It slid to a halt. The hair swung, heavy as cloth, as the head searched.

"I should have shut the door!" breathed Saxon.

Gilbert's breath rolled on her cheek. He whispered, "It is whole again!"

The Brogan's hair jerked; the arms pumped; it rattled through the dust, reaching forward; it raised the spetum in one hand.

The head turned slowly. Saxon held Gilbert, very still.

Suddenly the spetum clanged down, as the Brogan beat the blade on the floor; then the great weapon soared over the balustrade, dropping into the spotlit blackness below.

"It thinks we came to kill it!" hissed Saxon.

The Brogan rumbled to the balustrade and peered down between the little pillars. It pumped slowly, to a pink head on a stand. It reached up and lifted the head on to the broad top of the balustrade.

Gilbert's fingers knotted in Saxon's palm. The children knew the head's dreadful weight. The Brogan slid it along the balustrade then peered again through the pillars to where the spetum lay below. It reached behind itself and drew from the rags, the broken spear. Then it waited.

Gilbert's face moved whitely in the gloom.

The stone head gazed, shadows black in its eyes, daring them, it seemed to touch the spetum below.

Slowly, hating the whispering plastic, Saxon backed Gilbert around the pillar, into a gallery lit only by lights glowing over pictures.

"We need the spetum," she breathed. "There is nothing in this world to dig with." She waved the coffee bottle at the useless paintings.

"The Brogan will drop the head on us."

"I will lead the Brogan away. You will get the spetum."

"No!"

"Yes. You have the spear. Though I think there will be few spiders. Leave the scoop under this bench. I will leave the coffee. Go," she ordered gently.

"Where will I find you?" asked Gilbert in a tiny voice.

"On the stairs above this world."

He touched her hand and left.

Saxon paced back to the balcony. She rustled plastic and the Brogan heaved! with its hands on the floor, rattling towards her with sudden awful speed, slowed little, seemingly, by the dust.

Saxon fled among paintings. She ran through an arch not choked with grit. She glanced back, jogging, running suddenly, when the Brogan rolled too close, head dipping in the gloom, hair flowing; across its mouth, the spear-end.

Saxon sped on tiles with only a little grit grinding into her soles. The rattle sounded loud between narrow walls.

She ran faster. The dancing bags took her concentration, dragged her – ever-so-slightly – off balance.

She rushed on to a balcony. One foot skidded, hurling her sideways. The dagger rose from her fingers, flickering over the balustrade. She gasped as her head struck the floor. Lights burst in her skull, blinding her; deafening her; then she cried out as pain in her throat bent her head back.

Smiling down kindly was the bronze girl. The bronze boy laughed. The Brogan grunted and Saxon stared along the length of the spear that pinned her neck; at knuckles, yellow and hard-skinned like an ugly foot, and an arm, beautifully muscular; the hair curtained the face and body; and behind the body, rose curves of bone – once broken off; now replaced.

Sweat prickled on Saxon's cheeks. Could she move swiftly enough to dodge the thrust? The point caught her skin.

She crept her fingers on the tiles, ready to push. Her heart thudded sharply. Her breath dried her tongue.

Why did it wait?

"Why do you hate me?" gasped Saxon.

Stillness.

"I bring you food! Coffee! You wrote in the dust! I put coffee in the orange cup! I'm sorry to go into your room, but you weren't there! Why do you hate me!"

The needle point jerked into her neck.

Then the arm relaxed; the head turned; the spear withdrew and dropped as the creature pulled close to the children of bronze.

Saxon thrust against the tiles and ran; but no rattle followed. She slowed, and hopped to clean something from her foot. Something she had slipped on. Cheese.

A sound followed her. Blood stickied her throat.

The sound, drifting around the gallery walls, cooled her hate. The sound of woe. The Brogan weeping.

She found the coffee bottle and the scoop and grasped them like weapons. Without her spear and dagger she was naked; but for the moment, no enemies threatened.

She called.

She searched among split walls and fallen lights.

Scraping, and dust floating from an archway.

"Gilbert!"

"Saxon! I was beginning to worry!" His voice fell from high around the curve of the stair.

Saxon left the bottle, and went up with the scoop.

"It is very heavy!" gasped Gilbert, dumping the spetum. "There's blood on your neck!"

"I am correct, Gilbert. I have spoken to the Brogan. I think, maybe, it doesn't hate us." She lifted the end of the spetum, and together they swung the weapon deep into the grit.

"It has always hated us."

"It suffers," said Saxon, and work silenced her thoughts, and thud, said the spetum, scrape, said the spetum; dribble, said grit. Thud!

On.

Minutes.

In another world, green numbers changed.

Hours.

Resting. Eating bread and bacon mashed by Saxon's fall.

They used the scoop and hands to shovel grit down the stairs; and so much sneezing!

"It must be sleeptime!" gasped Gilbert, and Saxon smiled, for he was brown, every bit, except his eyes. And he grinned. Except his teeth. She touched the blood on her throat and rubbed it away, hardened with dust.

They gulped coffee as the lights went out. Paintings vanished into darkness. Only a single pin-prick glowed far away; and on the stair, the light above the tiny room.

They worked.

The grit wall broke and fell, exposing a

window; but Saxon thought the light had come from higher up; and anyway, even Gilbert could not squeeze through so narrow a window frame.

Often now, they retreated to the world below, to breathe and rest.

They uncovered a landing.

They wondered why less dust billowed around them. Grit broke away in cakes that they could lift and throw over the iron banister. The cakes were cool on their hands.

Then Gilbert said, after passing a lump to Saxon, "My hands are wet." And she threw the lump and looked. Her hands were wet.

The next stroke of the spetum exposed a windowsill. The windowsill, though difficult to see in the gloom, seemed dark with moisture.

Gilbert touched the sill, tipping his fingers to his tongue. "There is no taste." And they attacked with the spetum, piercing the grit above the sill.

The spetum went through, sliding, until they had little to hold.

Saxon's heart jumped.

"Pull!" she whispered, and they pulled, and the spetum's barbs caught, and they pulled again, hauling glass and lead on to the landing. Then they dropped the spetum, gasping, and fled down the stairs into the familiar darkness of the world below.

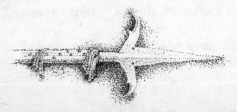

They crouched, shivering on a bench.

Shivering with cold.

Gilbert said, "Darkness! Dust and darkness! And cold! Outside is cold!" His teeth glinted. "There is no light!" And he curled into himself, shutting her out.

Saxon rose. "Come."

She left him to follow, or remain.

She went up the curve of the stairs to the landing.

Chill breath poured over her. Only in the freezer had she known real cold.

Beyond the windowsill – outside – something on the grit stirred.

In the darkness, Saxon could not see clearly.

She lifted the grit in both palms, and went down to stand beneath the light.

Chills of wonder added to her shivers.

In her hands, trembled a cluster of tiny green blades; and a ball of white, pea-sized, nodded on a stem. Drops of dusty water clung to it.

"Oh, Gilbert!" she breathed.

"Gilbert!"

Her voice soared. "Gilbert!"

He hurried, clinging to the banister, white-faced under his dusty mask.

She held her hands down to him. "Oh, Gilbert!" she whimpered. "Bellis perennis. Do you remember the book? A daisy, Gilbert! Dust and darkness? A daisy!" Tears escaped her eyelids.

Gilbert sank on to the landing. The grass and daisy trembled in his hands. He simply sat; and she sat with him, the little clump of life between them; weeping with awe; weeping with relief.

And because it was past sleeptime, and because they had worked so very hard, they dozed; then Saxon woke, her bones aching inside her bruised flesh. They carried the daisy to the bench, and slept again; and on Gilbert's lap, the daisy held its petals tightly shut.

She dreamed, Saxon.

Of daisies. Of daisies dotted white on the avalanche in CENTRAL HALL; daisies growing on pillars, with their tight ball-heads opened into little plates, each with a centre as yellow as yolk. Even in her sleep, Saxon questioned how she knew their colour, and she replied, Oh, I saw it in the encyclopaedia, Saxon. In the library. You do remember, don't you, Saxon? You do remember, don't you, Saxon? You do –

A daisy tickled her face.

The bench was gritty under her arm. Lights glowed. Something slid on her cheek, and her hand struck, spinning the thing away and she stood on the bench, snatching Gilbert's spear, striking down –

"Saxon!"

The spear flickered, entering the dust, bursting a –

Saxon lifted the blade, staring.

"It's a piece of paper."

"Saxon!" Gilbert spread his hands. "The daisy is gone!"

"The Brogan!" whispered Saxon. "It came creeping." She removed the paper from the spear.

"It could have killed us. Oh, look! I saw this in the Brogan's room! The Brogan has brought it to me! Oh, look! Oh, Gilbert – "

"What does it mean? It has written your name!"

"I don't know! I don't know." She sat limp in the dim-lit world, ignoring the dusty paintings and cracked walls, the thousand tricklings, and groaning stone columns.

Gilbert untied a bag from Saxon's belt, and they ate bacon sandwiches, well-squashed. From the other bag they nibbled cake crumbs. They finished the coffee.

"There is a toilet," said Gilbert. "That way."

They used the toilet, and washed their faces, especially their ears which were very dusty, and their feet. They did not wash all over, because the water was cold. Saxon put water in the coffee bottle.

She let the toilet door close behind her. Columns a span wide stood closely around.

She listened. Gilbert listened.

A group of women wept stone tears, hands appealing to the void beyond the balustrade. Spotlights divided the gloom. Cases glowed through dusty veils. Heads waited, balanced on their shadows, pretending the world was correct.

Above the world, something bumped.

"Is it a trembling?" whispered Gilbert.

"It is different."

"The sound of the spetum was like that."

"Yes." But the spetum lay on the staircase with cold air blowing over it, and the new sound came

94

muffled from above.

Gilbert looked at Saxon, waiting her command.

She nodded, and he stepped round a stone column.

She took a half-step to follow, but he strode back, his heel on her foot, and she jumped aside, but Gilbert stood still, head high, a length of spear reaching to his throat, and the Brogan, dreadful with silence.

Saxon didn't move.

The spear shifted, forcing Gilbert to walk backwards in a curve, away from the toilet, step by small step past the weeping women; and Saxon danced tense, clutching the bottle, Gilbert his spear held wide.

Clunk fell from above the far balcony. In the gallery below, Saxon glimpsed the animals, dumb in the dust.

She shuffled around a large painting wrecked on the arms of sculptured wrestlers. *Clunk*, and grit whispered. Saxon stared at the steel in Gilbert's throat. She dragged her eyes away, and saw the grit streaming down, full of rising dust, falling where Another lay.

Crash! A lump dropped, blasting dust between the balustrade's pillars, and the Brogan jerked, pushing swiftly on the floor with one hand, daring Gilbert to fall, Saxon guiding him past violins; the bottle a nuisance – or a weapon.

In the Brogan's room, the red bench pressed on their backs. Raw heat from the fire blazed at Saxon's leg. The spear struck, knocking Gilbert's blade to the floor, then leaped back pinning his skin into a little pit-shape in his neck.

The Brogan balanced on whatever rattled under its rags, and pushed the door shut with its hand.

Ending the sound above the world.

Leaving Saxon's thoughts in silence.

She stared at the Brogan, with its hair, dusty fair, motionless as granite. She saw the bones sticking up from its back, dark bones, as worn as the haft of Gilbert's spear. She shuddered at the thought of touching them. The head jerked towards her.

And she shuddered more and longer, for she had always thought of the Brogan as a living creature –

She recognized that the bones were the handles of a porter's barrow.

She decided the Brogan was listening. The *clunk!* fell faint in the room. The heater blazed on Saxon's leg. Why was she here with Gilbert? Did the sound have meaning? Meaning to the Brogan?

The noise stopped.

The spear moved in Gilbert's throat as the Brogan sighed.

Then it withdrew the spear, and lunged! at Gilbert! at Saxon! sending them tumbling over the bench. The door banged, and when they untangled from each other and looked, the Brogan was gone. Saxon ran back round the bench for Gilbert's spear, but it had vanished with the Brogan.

"I have my dagger!" gasped Gilbert.

"It has both spears! It is very strong. The Brogan is made of wood."

"What do you mean?"

"The Brogan is wood and metal. Two metal wheels. It is not alive."

"Of course it is – "

"I saw, Gilbert! Part of it is a barrow."

"It has arms like yours!"

Breath heaved among Saxon's ribs. "I am being stupid!" she wept. "I do not wish to know! I will not – I will not remember!"

Gilbert held her. And she sobbed, destroying her thoughts with misery.

"It is the stone," she whimpered. "Falling on the steps beyond the great doors. And the shoe, bright as blood – and trees, alive like the daisy is alive, and the ceiling of the world shining, oh! with glorious light!"

She pushed suddenly, out of Gilbert's embrace and ran back round the bench.

"Look." Saxon lifted the daisy from the sink. "She has washed it."

"She?"

A sigh trembled over her tongue.

"Yes," she said. "She."

The sink vibrated under her palm. Saxon sped to the door, and pressed down the handle. "It won't open!"

A moan filled the world. The tap juddered; water gushed under the floor. The orange cup danced.

Gilbert tugged the door handle.

"Use your dagger!" said Saxon, but the lock clicked and the door jerked inwards, a spear finding Gilbert's chest. Saxon swung the bottle, striking the spear down; Gilbert's foot thrust, and the Brogan spun. The children ran; avoiding dust that boiled up from below the balcony. They hurried through looming archways; they sped along a corridor then out, suddenly, into a brown fog glowing with chandeliers.

"We are above CENTRAL HALL!" cried Saxon.

"Look! Look!" Gilbert shook her arm. Stone ground on stone. Pillars fell from the balcony which supported the organ. The organ pipes leaned at a dreadful angle, squealing, then toppled below the chandeliers, spearing the dust that buried the orrery, bursting the orrery's dome, exploding glass, setting the chandeliers swinging in a rush of air.

And a noise too awful for human ears screamed above the children. Dust rushed at them, and they fled through the ruins of the worlds clutching their heads.

They ran as they had never run before. A crack sped across the tiles and they leapt over it. Paintings shook on the walls, and shadows jittered as lights trembled. Bulbs banged, darkening the floor, scattering glass. A wall sagged, dropping paintings and plaster, white dust bursting into Saxon's face; and a noise so terrible that the children held their ears – the precious coffee bottle dropped – a noise like the end of the world, and Saxon knew the roof above CENTRAL HALL had collapsed, and the crashing and rending went on and on until there was nowhere to run…

They stumbled against a door. They shut it behind them and fell trembling into a corner.

Around them, the world cried out in many voices.

"Gilbert." He pressed close. "We must find the light. We must go outside."

He hugged her arm.

They sat, Saxon afraid to face the destruction; terrified of outside. Then she remembered the daisy. It had come from outside. She held Gilbert tightly.

"Why did the Brogan keep us in its room?" he whispered.

"So we wouldn't leave," said Saxon. "Come," she whispered. She helped him up, and they stood holding hands. She embraced him suddenly with both arms, and his little hands clasped her back. Then she opened the door and they ran into the brown mist.

"That way!" gasped Gilbert and immediately coughed.

They stumbled over pieces of ceiling. They trod on paintings. The fog rolled, full of soft light. Saxon wondered where the light was coming from, because all around lay the wreckage of bulbs and glass tubes.

"Here!" said Gilbert.

Saxon fumbled through a familiar archway. "Now we shall see!" She strode up two steps clutching the iron rail, but the rail curved under her hand and ended in a ragged point. Stones had smashed through it, carrying the rail and part of the staircase to the floor below. Grit slithered above her, and Saxon pushed Gilbert back. A massive lump of plaster bounced down the stair towards them, plunging through the hole, crashing, dust exploding.

They ran. Then they walked. More noise made them look back, then they hurried away hopelessly; the staircase had collapsed.

They wandered, avoiding the crack in the floor, avoiding walls that leaned. They coughed, and blinked away dust.

The air was cold and pushed gently around the children, heaving the fog; but Gilbert said nothing, and Saxon sighed, for their world was destroyed, and cold mattered not at all when existence was about to end.

Then the worlds rested, silent, and dust drifted, exploring the ruins.

The children walked under an archway and stared on to the wrecked balconies; they stared at the heavy brown fog glowing as though lit from above, and – puzzled – Saxon stepped close to the balcony's torn edge where stone women had once wept. She coughed, and coughed again.

It was a pleasant light. Something caught her ankle.

She gasped. "Gilbert!" she whispered. She crouched.

"Help me!" And she reached down, over the edge, and gripped the Brogan's wrist; for it was the Brogan's awful hand that held her ankle, and the creature hung dumbly with nothing but death below.

"Hold her!" gasped Saxon. Gilbert's fingers sought the Brogan's arm, biting tight. "Pull!" The barrow dangled at a strange angle from among the rags.

"It's too heavy!" cried Gilbert.

"Give us your other hand," urged Saxon. Her tears ran freely. The Brogan's head tilted up at them and the hair fell away slightly, exposing an eye as blue as Gilbert's. The arm moved, but flopped between the elbow and wrist.

"Try to pull yourself up! Keep hold of my ankle! Oh, please pull!" Saxon stared. The blue eye was wet with tears. A grunt came from behind the hair. The eye moved, looking around, and the head shifted as if to say, "There is nothing left." And the eye looked past Saxon at Gilbert, blinking, squeezing away the tears, then it found Saxon. She was certain the eye was smiling, quite sanely, then it blinked again, once, very slowly, like a loving thank-you; the head nodded slightly, and the grip on Saxon's ankle was released. Gilbert cried out.

"No!" gasped Saxon, but their fingers were not strong enough and the beautiful arm slid from their grasp, thick hand momentarily in theirs, then the Brogan was gone, dropping into the darkness where light would never shine again.

And they lay weeping, Saxon and Gilbert,

weeping for something found then lost in a heart-beat, and Saxon suddenly knew many things. A great stone falling. A young woman on the steps of the museum. The stone touching her face as it came down, striking her legs. A red shoe, and two children obeying instructions spoken only a moment earlier. "Get inside. Whatever happens don't come out!" And she had fled with Gilbert inside, and whatever happened she hadn't come out. Despite the screams, she hadn't come out.

Despite people leaving as dust piled over the windows; deeper day by day, week by week, month by month, she hadn't come out. And she had forgotten the screams, and the fearful thing that crawled among the shadows weeping and moaning.

From above, a new light danced, cutting angles in the air.

"Gilbert!" Saxon wiped her face.

The children crouched. Gilbert's dagger tilted in his hand.

"Come!" whispered Saxon, and she led him over the crumbling tiles, around the balcony, towards where Another lay.

"Denby! Sergeant Denby!"

The children stopped. Saxon's blood flowed cold and Gilbert shrank against her. "It is the voice of God!" he whimpered.

"It is the voice of Another!" gasped Saxon.

"I'm going down!" said the voice. "Be ready to pull me up! I don't think there's much chance of finding him alive –" The light flickered across Saxon's eyes. "What – Holy Mother of God!"

The light blinded Saxon.

She stood up, Gilbert beside her.

"There are two kids down here!"

A white figure descended to the floor. It came towards them, tall and shining gently in the light from the dust. It stopped before them, and knelt.

Through a window in the white helmet Saxon looked on the face of a man.

"Where did you kids come from! How long have you been here!" He gaped. He reached out and touched them on the shoulder.

"We have been here four years, eighty-five days," said Saxon. "I am Saxon. This is my brother, Gilbert. Saxon and Gilbert Brogan. Our mother is dead."

THE HAUNTED SAND

Hugh Scott

"Murder, Frisby! Murder on the beach!"

There's something creepy in the churchyard. There's something deathly down on the sand. Darren feels it, Frisby hears it, George thinks it's a bit of a laugh. But there's nothing funny about murder...

"Intriguing ingredients abound: a haunted church; fearful chases; ghostly weeping; skulls; bronze helmets; gems and The Black Death... Rendellesque subtleties of storyline build to an unforeseen climax."
The Times Educational Supplement

THE TRIPLE SPIRAL
Stephanie Green

The wind rose to a howl and in it was the baying of the infernal hounds. The reeds hissed like snakes. Moddy Dhu crouched, snarling, his teeth bared, his eyes evil, red slits.

When Sonia and her family move into an isolated windmill in Norfolk, they find the area rife with legend and superstition. Preoccupied with their own domestic tensions, the Carrs have little time for stories about a Moon Goddess, a demon dog or a terrible flood. Gradually, though, these "myths" start to take on a very real and terrifying significance...

"This first novel, multi-layered, complex, elegantly structured as it is, manages to grip almost from the first page... A beautifully constructed ghost story."
Books for Your Children

"The scenes of family life are original and provocative."
The Times Educational Supplement

THE LAST CHILDREN

Gudrun Pausewang

It's the beginning of the summer holidays and the Bennewitzs are on their way to visit grandparents in the mountains. Suddenly, there's a blinding light in the sky – and the Bennewitzs are on the road to hell...

Shocking, distressing, brutally honest, this book has already profoundly affected thousands of readers in Germany. Read it and it will change you too.

"This disturbing book shouldn't be limited to the teenage market but should be compulsory reading for most adults, especially those in positions of power."
Judy Allen, The Sunday Times

THICKER THAN WATER
Penelope Farmer

"Help me," the voice said. "Help me."

Becky and Will are cousins. But apart from blood ties they seem to have little in common: Will, skinny and withdrawn; Becky, plump and forthright. So when Will comes to live with her family in the heart of Derbyshire mining country, Becky is hardly overjoyed. What's more, it soon becomes clear that something disturbing is haunting Will...

"Striking and well-conceived ... with a fitting and very moving climax... Bears comparison with the best of her early books, *Charlotte Sometimes*."
The Times Literary Supplement

"Penelope Farmer's gripping tale of supernatural possession is as convincing as it is genuinely frightening."
Scotland on Sunday

SHADOW IN HAWTHORN BAY
Janet Lunn

Softly she began to sing in Gaelic a song for the dying, and as she sang she stepped off the rock into the bay. She walked out until she stood waist-deep in the water.

"I am coming, mo gradach, I am coming to be where you are."

Fifteen-year-old Highland girl Mary Urquhart has the gift of second sight. One spring morning in 1815 she hears the voice of her beloved cousin Duncan calling to her from three thousand miles away in upper Canada and knows that somehow she must go to him. It is to prove a long and perilous journey, however, and Mary encounters much heartbreak and adversity before her quest finally comes to an end.

"Memorable ... haunting... In one sense this is a ghost-novel – but it is also true to human behaviour."
Naomi Lewis, The Observer

"Janet Lunn tells a compelling tale."
The Times Educational Supplement

DEEP HOLY JOE AND THE BALLAD OF THE BAND

Michael Gizzie

All night long the bands went on and off.
The judges were smiles and laughs,
marking points and signing autographs.
Holy Joe watched the faces.
The last chord of the last band died.
He watched his band take their places,
and went alongside.
The band took the stage...

In a suburb, somewhere, five school leavers form
a band: Sam, the strummer; Mike, the drummer;
Ace, the singer; "Brass-Finger" Bob on sax and
Itchy Fred on keyboards. Holding them together
is Deep Holy Joe, bassist and guru. This colourful
blues ballad is their story.

TIME PIPER
Delia Huddy

"The door of the lab burst open. Something came out; something at floor level. It was lucky that Luke was not in the corridor or he might have been knocked out… Whatever it was came from the laboratory in a living torrent of bodies and swept down the corridor."

From the day he meets the beautiful, remote mysterious Hare, Luke's life is turned upside down. But what can be the connection between this strange lost girl and Tom Humboldt the brilliant inventor of a Time Machine? The answer, it seems, lies in the past…

"Very ingenious… A very good book."
The Standard

"Very perceptive … not really sci-fi but a love story."
Peter Hunt, The Times Literary Supplement

MORE WALKER PAPERBACKS
For You to Enjoy